W9-BVB-447

Boogers and Boo-Daddies

John F. Blair, Publisher
Winston-Salem, North Carolina

Boogers and Boo-Daddies

The Best of Blair's Ghost Stories

Selected by
the Staff of John F. Blair, Publisher

Published by John F. Blair, Publisher

*The paper in this book meets the guidelines
for permanence and durability of the
Committee on Production Guidelines for
Book Longevity of the Council on Library Resources.*

Decorative elements on pages i, ii, iii, and
all chapter beginnings are taken from the jacket image—
Boo by Michael Catfish Man Suter / Acrylic on wood painting

Library of Congress Cataloging-in-Publication Data

Boogers and boo-daddies : the best of Blair's ghost stories / edited by the staff
of John F. Blair, Publisher.
p.   cm.
ISBN 0-89587-296-X
1. Ghosts—Southern States. I. John F. Blair, Publisher.
BF1472.U6B66 2004
133.1'0975—dc22
2003020783

Design by Debra Long Hampton

Contents

Introduction

On a small circle in a commercial section of Winston-Salem, North Carolina, sits a nondescript brick building on a shaggy lawn. A young man not long out of college came to work as an editor there. One of his duties was reading the book manuscripts submitted for publication at the company. Proud of his education and self-assured in his sensibilities, he took a certain joy in the task.

"Hey, look at this!" he would say. "Here's a guy who compares himself to Faulkner."

Or he'd say, "This lady claims her poems are popular with everyone in her circle at church. I bet that's a tough crowd."

If he came across a sentence of particularly awkward construction, he'd go from office to office reading it aloud to his co-workers.

When he was in a generous mood, he rejected manuscripts with a form letter notable for its terseness. When he wasn't so kindly disposed, he threw them in the trash and didn't reply at all.

It so happened that the young man was given the desk of the company's late founder, known as one of the last great gentlemen in publishing. In fact, not many years previous, the aged gentleman had been found dead at that desk, slumped over the unruly piles of paper residing there. "A neat desk is a sign of a sick mind" read a placard posted for all to see. The young man took it down.

The new editor had been running roughshod over submissions for two or three months when he arrived one morning to find that a manuscript had been pulled out of his trash and set on his desk. Atop it lay an old-fashioned onionskin sheet that hadn't been run through a computer printer but apparently typed on an ancient manual, the lowercase *a* appearing half a line above the other letters. "Dear Mrs. McGee," the letter began, "While your novel does not fit with my current line of books, I wanted to tell you that it brought me several hours of pleasure." It went on for three paragraphs, discovering value where the young man had seen none.

The following morning, and the morning after that, he found that more submissions had been similarly rescued from the trash. At first, he paraded the onionskin letters around to his co-workers, but as a week passed, then another, he began to feel chided by the writer's generosity and grace. He asked, then demanded to know, who it was who felt they could do his job better than he did it. When no one admitted responsibility, he searched the supply cabinet for the onionskin sheets and the dark corners of the building for a discarded Royal or Smith-Corona. He accused the woman from the cleaning service of pilfering his trash, then started taking his can and emptying it directly into the dumpster. But every morning would bring more submissions risen from the grave.

Though it would make a better story, it would be disingenuous to claim that the young man ran screaming into the night or that he began to see visions or hear voices. But he did leave the company within a year, returning home to live with his parents and work dead-end jobs. Perhaps it is he at the carwash sponging your hood or at the late-night window handling your burger and fries.

No more onionskin sheets have shown themselves at the office, though the staff does occasionally come across some gravy-stained napkins and unexplained takeout boxes from the K & W Cafeteria, the old gentleman's favorite.

Is the above story true? No self-respecting folklorist would answer that question. "It's true as far as I know," they'd hedge, or "That story has been handed down through several generations," or "It came to me from a respectable person whose word I trust." Or they'd take refuge behind the old Mark Twain saw: "It may be only a legend, a tradition. It may have happened, it may not have happened. But it could have happened." Charles Harry Whedbee, the beloved raconteur of North Carolina's Outer Banks, had a couplet he liked to recite when someone inquired about the veracity of his tales: "I do not say what I know to be, / I only tell what was told to me." Whedbee saw his stories as being divided into three categories: those he knew to be true, those he believed to be true, and those he knew to be fabrications. But he would never say which stories were which. Many of his readers guessed—and they generally guessed wrong.

Worrying oneself about the truthfulness of folklore misses the point anyway. Folk tales are intended partly to inform and partly to carry on tradition but mainly to entertain. But that is not to say they should be dismissed as lightweight fare. Folklore, as the saying goes, is the true mother of history.

You hold in your hands a collection of twenty folk tales, one each from the twenty collections published by a certain firm on a small circle in a medium-sized Southern town. They are arranged in the order in which they were published. The oldest collections came out nearly forty years ago; all remain in print today. You'll note a general progression in style from the old-time tales of Charles Harry Whedbee to the more modern tellings of Elizabeth Robertson Huntsinger, Daniel W. Barefoot, and the husband-and-wife team of Randy Russell and Janet Barnett. You'll also notice that some of the folklorists have a strong regional identity—like Fred T. Morgan and the Uwharrie Mountains—or a special interest in a certain type of lore—like Nancy Roberts and her pirate tales. Some folklorists capitalize on their long association with a particular place—like Nancy Rhyne and the South Carolina Low Country—while others are relative newcomers captivated by a signature place—like Charles Edwin Price and the mountains of upper East Tennessee.

This collection is a tribute to those folklorists who deserve a large share of the credit for keeping the company founded by gentleman publisher John F. Blair in business for half a century.

Boogers and Boo-Daddies

Lady in Distress

from *Legends of the Outer Banks and Tar Heel Tidewater*
by Charles Harry Whedbee

Many and varied are the tales that are told of the lady Theodosia Burr Alston. Some are dull, and some exciting, but all of them end in tragedy. That she was an actual historical figure, there is not the slightest doubt. That she was a most pitiful and appealing person is also apparent. For years her fate was unknown and was the subject of much speculation, but, with the perspective of time, the pieces of the puzzle seem to fall into place. With the corroboration of several deathbed confessions by persons who should have known whereof they spoke, one can now deduce a fairly accurate picture of the beautiful, headstrong, and star-crossed lady.

Theodosia Burr was born to Aaron Burr and his wife in the city of Albany and raised in New York, then the capital of the young United States. While she was still a small child, her mother died, and Aaron determined to be both mother and father to her. He set out with the avowed intention of creating in his daughter his ideal of what the perfect woman should be. He himself was active in the highest circles of the national government of his country. His ambition and his political vision seemed to be unlimited, and his rise into political fortune seemed almost meteorlike in its dramatic brilliance.

Into the rearing of his child, this near-genius poured all the love and devotion he had felt for his wife, and out of his loneliness he drew the strength and dedication to do a superlative job. Burr envisioned his daughter as the perfect wife for some lucky man. She was to be so highly trained as to be a model of intelligence and charm, completely without the vacuity that characterized so many belles of the day. She was to be warm and understanding and able to be a real helpmeet to her husband at any and all levels of his life. Latin and Greek Burr taught her, as well as dancing and the harpsichord. She was as good at a game of chess as she was at working a pretty sampler.

Theodosia's eagerness in this training was matched only by her father's delight in her progress. She literally worshiped her talented father and wanted with all her young heart to be everything he wanted her to be. By the time she was twelve years old, this precocious child was already an accomplished hostess. By the age of sixteen, she was presiding at many of the most important receptions and other functions in the nation's capital.

Many suitors paid court to this remarkable girl. The scions of wealthy and influential families tried their best to win her hand in marriage; but to Theo, none of them could compare with her brilliant father. He outshone them all.

Then she met young Joseph Alston. Son of one of the finest families in South Carolina, he was reared in a tradition not unlike her own. He was intensely interested in politics and government. His future seemed bright and assured, and without doubt he loved Theodosia with all his heart. Youth called unto youth, and the distinguished troth was plighted.

In one of the most dazzling social functions of this country, Theodosia Burr became the bride of the Honorable Joseph Alston. After their wedding trip, the couple removed to South Carolina, where, true to the promise of his youth, Alston rose rapidly in the political world and became governor. One son was born, and he was promptly named Aaron Burr Alston. According to all reports, he was as lovely and charming a child as one could well imagine.

Then the shadow of tragedy began to move across the scene, and the family fortunes fell on darker days. Aaron Burr, outstanding young statesman that he was, became involved in a great political scandal. Alexander

Hamilton, another giant of the times, opposed Burr at every turn and seemed to be his nemesis. Burr and Thomas Jefferson were opposing candidates for the presidency of the United States, and the contest had ended in a tie vote. Hamilton redoubled his efforts against Burr, who, strangely, made no concerted effort to overcome the tie with Jefferson. Jefferson and Burr, therefore, each had seventy-three electoral votes, with Hamilton doing all in his power to bring about Burr's defeat and Burr remaining strangely silent. Ballot after ballot was taken, and, finally, on the thirty-sixth ballot the tie was broken. Thomas Jefferson became the third President of the United States, taking office in the year 1801.

Burr remained silent no longer. Bitter in his disappointment and goaded by the memory of Hamilton's opposition, he challenged Hamilton to a duel to the death. Hamilton did not want the duel and had it delayed several times, but Burr was adamant, and the two finally met on the "field of honor" on July 11, 1804, at the little town of Weehawken, New Jersey.

Now remember, Hamilton was the statesman who had insisted on the construction of lighthouses along the North Carolina coast. The lighthouse at Hatteras had been the direct result of his efforts and influence. To this day, many of the old-timers refer to it as "Hamilton's light."

As Hamilton and Burr descended from their carriages in the dim dawn and took their places on the greensward, the seconds asked each if the duel could not be averted and the matter settled without the drawing of blood. Burr shook his head, and Hamilton remained silent. As the signals were given, each of the antagonists raised and aimed his pistol. At the final signal, both fired almost simultaneously. Hamilton's shot went wide; but Burr fired with deadly accuracy, and Hamilton fell, mortally wounded. Thus was brought to an abrupt end the career of one of the most courageous and able statesmen of the young republic, and the Outer Banks lost one of its first and best friends.

A shocked and outraged citizenry demanded retribution for this act. Burr heard the political pack in full cry for his public life.

Rumors began to circulate that the onetime Revolutionary colonel was engaged in trying to stir up rebellion in the territories west of the Appalachian Mountains. Quickly the word spread that the former patriot was now bent upon the destruction of the country he had served.

History leaves us no room to doubt that Colonel Aaron Burr did, indeed, nourish ambitious and fantastic dreams of a secession of Kentucky and Tennessee from the United States, as well as a revolt of the Mississippi

Territory and of the huge area later to be known as Alabama, Louisiana, and part of Texas, which had only recently been acquired by the young republic in the Louisiana Purchase.

Burr envisioned himself as the chief executive, possibly even the king, of this new nation, with the capital to be located in the city of New Orleans. Here he would preside (or reign) over a court of such brilliance as to put to shame the rather plain surroundings of President Thomas Jefferson in Washington. Even a military campaign to wrest Mexico and Florida from the Spanish was considered. Colonel Burr's vaulting ambition knew no bounds, and he was most indiscreet in talking about his dreams to people who he thought might be helpful.

Word of Burr's plans soon reached President Jefferson and the members of his Cabinet, and the time seemed ideal to lay a trap to catch the killer of Hamilton. Thus it was that when Burr took a boat from Pittsburgh to travel down the Ohio and Mississippi Rivers for New Orleans, one John Graham, an agent of Jefferson, trailed Burr in the hope of catching him in some overt act of treason.

The further south Burr progressed, the greater became the public support for his plans. This so alarmed Jefferson that he sent word ahead that the firebrand was to be arrested on sight for high treason.

Arrested in the Mississippi Territory, Burr willingly gave himself up to the civil authorities, claiming that he only intended the good of the western territories and the defeat and confusion of royalist Spain.

Tried in a Mississippi Territory court, Burr was acquitted of the charge of treason by a three-judge panel and released. Regardless of this, he was rearrested by federal troops several days later, put in irons, and transported the long, weary miles to Richmond, Virginia, where President Jefferson was determined he should stand trial again for high treason— this time in a federal court.

Once again the brilliant little colonel was tried for high treason and for levying acts of war against the United States. Once again he was acquitted. One of the great landmarks of American law was erected here when John Marshall ruled in the pivotal decision of the case that "treason" and "levying war" against one's own country could be established only by an "overt act" in the first instance and by an "assemblage of men in preparation for battle" in the second. Thus was substantial justice achieved in that Burr was not convicted of treason, for the charges had been laid mainly because of the fatal duel with Hamilton. Dueling was the established order of the day, and to have perverted the law by punishing Burr for treason when what he had done was to kill a promising statesman would have been legal hypocrisy of the lowest kind. The orderly, precise mind of Marshall perceived this, and legal history was made.

Although his life was spared, Aaron Burr's political star had set. Broken in health and in spirit, he went into voluntary exile in England, where he stayed until the year 1812. Although he had been tried for treason, Burr loved his country, and when the clouds of war began to threaten and it became apparent that England would try to retake her former colony by force, Burr betook himself back to his beloved America and offered his services to her. Once again he attempted to regain a portion of his former influence and power as a leader in the political forums, but he met with rebuff after rebuff, and his failures made him heartsick.

In South Carolina, his daughter Theodosia had suffered for him during all his trials and misfortunes. As soon as she heard that he was coming back to this country, she made plans to visit him in New York. With all her heart she believed that she could cheer and encourage him at this time when he desperately needed someone to lean on. Her husband was still governor of South Carolina and perhaps could be of some help. Plans for the visit were progressing but came to a complete halt when her only son, the handsome little Aaron Burr Alston, fell ill with the fever and died in her arms in June 1812.

This loss left Theodosia prostrate in both mind and body. For a while her life as well as her sanity were despaired of. Youth and natural vigor prevailed, though, and she began to mend. Although still terribly depressed in spirit, she began to eat and to move about her former duties. By late fall of that same year she was beginning to talk once again of her desire to see her father in New York. She felt that she now needed him almost as much as he needed her.

In the hope that it might revive her spirits and make her once again the vivacious and charming young woman she had once been, her husband made arrangements for her to take the trip to New York to see her father. Although the War of 1812 was raging at the time and British warships were patrolling the entire coast, these were still the days of chivalry in warfare, and Governor Alston knew that any ship engaged on such a mission as his would be passed unharmed through the British blockade, particularly if it carried a letter from the governor himself addressed to the honor of the British navy.

Thus, in December 1812, the good ship *Patriot* was commissioned and sailed, unarmed, from the harbor of Georgetown en route to New York. Aboard were the lady Theodosia Burr Alston and her personal maid. In her luggage was a beautiful oil portrait of herself which she had had painted and which she intended to give to her father. As she left Georgetown, Theodosia seemed more animated and excited than she had in many months. Already the trip seemed to be doing her good. The portrait was hung on the wall of her private cabin, and the young traveler was made comfortable by her devoted maid.

The *Patriot* was not many days out of Georgetown when, sure enough, she was hailed and stopped by British men-of-war. An inspection party came aboard, and the British commander was presented with the letter of Governor Alston requesting safe passage for his wife through the blockade. As a courtesy to the lady and to the governor of South Carolina, the *Patriot* was not even searched but was permitted to continue on her way and was wished Godspeed on her trip to New York.

Northward the *Patriot* sailed and into threatening weather. She passed Cape Hatteras, plainly marked by Hamilton's light, under shortened canvas; and as she left the light on the larboard quarter, the storm increased. For two days she lay hove-to behind a drogue and waited for the storm to blow itself out. By the evening of the third day the wind had subsided, and the sea was somewhat calmer; but the sky was still heavily overcast, and the captain had no idea just where he might be off the North Atlantic coast. With shortened sail and with lookouts at the masthead and in the chains, the *Patriot* cautiously probed her way through the darkness.

"Sail ho," came the cry from the masthead, "broad off the larboard beam." The helmsman and all others on deck immediately turned to the left and scanned the darkness. Just about broadside off the larboard side of the ship was a light that apparently could only mean another ship—a ship that could probably give them their exact position, no matter whether she was British or American. They had letters of safe conduct from the one and political identity with the other. Moreover, the light was barely moving; and its slow, easy rolling indicated to them that the lighted ship was in all probability lying at anchor.

Anxious for a chance to verify his position, the captain of the *Patriot* recalled his watch from the chains, ordered his ship brought about, and headed in the direction of the light. Not wanting to take the risk of missing her, he ordered the *Patriot* to proceed under full sail and at best speed.

A bow wave formed under the forefoot of the trim little craft, and her wake gurgled from the speed of her passage. Not until they were within hailing distance of the presumed friendly light did the captain and crew realize to their horror that they were in the breakers. They had fallen prey to the old, old trick of the land pirates—the pirates of Nags Head.

Hard aground rammed the *Patriot* on the outer bar in a welter of surf. Harder aground she lunged with each succeeding wave, more desperately and hopelessly lost. As the masts, under the pressure of the wind on full canvas, snapped off even with the deck, the mariners heard a new and more horrible sound. It was the screaming and cursing of the pirates as they put off through the surf in their small boats, not to rescue but to pillage and to kill. Up and over the sides of the helpless vessel they came, as motley and desperate a crew as can be imagined, but brave and cunning fighters every one. Up and down the decks of the *Patriot* they fought with the officers and men of the vessel until the scuppers of the doomed ship ran with blood. No sooner was a man cut down, whether pirate or sailor, than he was dumped overboard. In one awful half-hour every officer and seaman of the ship's company was ruthlessly murdered.

Theodosia, emerging from her cabin in fright when the *Patriot* had first run aground, watched in horrified disbelief. Her faithful maid was seized and thrown heartlessly overboard to the gathering sharks already tearing savagely in an orgy of blood lust at everything in the water. She went without a scream, without a word, without an outcry of any sort— her eyes fixed steadily upon those of her lovely young mistress. Then the pirates—dirks and swords red with blood—turned toward Theodosia, who stood cowering against the little superstructure of the cabin.

Already weakened by past sorrows and reeling from the sight of so many heartless acts of murder, the gentle mind of Theodosia Burr Alston took refuge in insanity. From that moment forward, and for as long as she lived, Theodosia was insane.

The land pirates, as have many primitive people before them since time began, respected that insanity. Moreover, they respected the person of Theodosia Burr Alston as one especially touched of God. Thus they feared to harm her, afraid of instant and violent retribution from above.

Gently, almost lovingly, they handed her down into a waiting surfboat and took her to shore. She took with her only one possession: the handsome oil portrait of herself which she had intended as a gift for her father.

The land pirates took the demented young woman into their homes.

From home to home she went as the months passed, always welcome but free to go or stay as her childlike fancy led her. The simple Bankers cared for her as though she were a daughter and saw to it that she lacked nothing that they could provide. She never tried to leave the island, never tried to run away. A vacant look held those lovely eyes, once sparkling with so much intelligence. To all greetings, all inquiries, her one reply was, "I am going to visit my father in New York." In her favorite fishing cottage where she stayed most often, the oil portrait hung at the place of honor over the mantel in the main room. It had replaced the shell of a huge horseshoe crab her hosts had formerly kept there. Often and for long minutes she would stand and stare at the picture as if trying to remember what it was and what significance it held for her. Always she would end such a scrutiny with a puzzled shake of her head and a weary sigh.

Thus the days passed, and the months, and the years. Some days were happy and some were periods of deep, black depression. Our castaway remained reasonably healthy, but there was no apparent improvement in her mental condition. After the last of the pirates had died or moved away, the fishermen took up the care of this pitiful woman and provided for her to the best of their ability. Theirs were acts of love and pity, rather than fear, and she was treated with unfailing kindness and generosity.

Many years later when Theodosia was an old, old woman and sick abed, Dr. William G. Poole, from Elizabeth City, whose kindly habit it was to visit the Outer Banks at intervals, came by the cottage where she was then staying. The doctor had treated her several times in the past without hope or expectation of fee. Often he had admired the oil portrait over the mantel and had wondered about its origin. Theodosia's hosts had offered him the portrait on several occasions, but he had always refused.

On this night, when once again the winds were wailing in their lonesome fury and the waves were beginning to pound in ever-increasing force up and onto the beach, the doctor had given Theodosia a mild sedative, and she was apparently asleep, completely relaxed and snoring gently. As the doctor turned to go, the head of the household took the portrait down from the wall and held it out to him. "Take it, doctor," the fisherman said. "It is little enough to give you for all the times you have helped her. If she were in her right mind, I know she would insist on your having it. Maybe you can sell it in Elizabeth City or in Norfolk. Take it as your fee."

Even as the good doctor shook his head in refusal, Theodosia leaped from her bed and, with a piercing shriek, snatched the picture from the hands of the fisherman. "It is mine. It is mine," she screamed. "You know I am going to visit my father in New York, and this is to be his picture—his picture of his Theo."

Grasping the portrait to her breast, she then ran out of the room so quickly that they could not detain her—out into the storm and down toward the pounding surf. In vain they followed—the doctor, the fisherman, and his wife and children—to try to prevent her injury. Theodosia disappeared into the driving mist and spume of a howling, raging wind. They never saw her again.

Theodosia's body was never found. The ocean had claimed her for its own. The deep prints of her running feet led down to the sea's edge but did not return. Next day, however, at high tide, the portrait was found just a short distance down the shore from where Theodosia had last been seen. All agreed that it should be given to the doctor. He reluctantly took it and promised to see if he could have it identified. The lady in the picture was obviously a person of wealth and breeding. The gown in which she was portrayed had an expensive look, and the few jewels were in excellent taste.

No sooner had the doctor gotten it back to the city than numerous people began to recognize it as being an excellent likeness of the lost Theodosia. Contact was made with the Burr family, who were told about the picture. Several members of the family made a special trip south to see it. They, too, identified the girl in the portrait as none other than the wife of the governor of South Carolina, the ill-fated Theodosia Burr Alston.

The finding of the portrait made all the newspapers of the day. Then three old men of the sea were reported, on separate occasions and in different cities, to have made deathbed confessions that they had taken part in the looting of a ship lured onto the Outer Banks between Christmas and New Year's in the year 1812. Each of them confessed in penitence that all the ship's company had been killed, that one young woman had been thrown to the sharks, and that the mind of another had been taken by God.

The portrait was treasured by Dr. Poole as long as he lived and was kept in his home. At his death it was inherited by his granddaughter, Mrs. John P. Overman, also of Elizabeth City.

Today the battered but still beautiful portrait has been preserved for those to whom it rightfully belongs, the American people. It hangs now in a place of honor in the Macbeth Art Gallery in New York City, where it is proudly identified as the young Mrs. Alston. Thus has Theodosia's portrait finally completed its journey to the town for which it was destined.

Is it more than just a coincidence that the slayer of the creator of Cape Hatteras Light should, in turn, lose his most precious possession, his only child, to the false lights displayed on those same Outer Banks? Whether this wild and beautiful region struck back in revenge for the senseless killing of one of its first and greatest friends is, of course, beyond pondering. Many people will assure you that if you walk the Nags Head beach during the dreary season between Christmas and New Year's; if you choose a time when the sky is overcast and the wind whines up from the wildness of the North Atlantic and blows wraiths of spume and spindrift along the beaches, you may see Theodosia. She will not harm you. She was always a gentle person. There she walks, they say, looking—ever looking—for that handsome portrait she longs to carry to her father in New York.

The Hatchet-Swinging Fire

from *Ghost Tales of the Uwharries*
by Fred T. Morgan

Thaddeus, an orphaned mountain boy, had taken up residence in the old Moser cabin in a wild cove of the Uwharries, up from the Yadkin River. Not so much from a fondness for isolation as from a desire for independence did he fix up the place enough to see him through the winter. Old man Morrison and one of his sons had helped him throw new poles across the roof, board up the holes in the walls, and repair the fallen stone chimney. He had worked for the Morrisons during the summer and fall. With his meager earnings he had bought and traded himself into possession of a long-barreled gun and a few steel traps with which he hoped to spend a profitable winter season.

Folks had warned him against it. "Won't do for you to stay up there alone all winter, son," they said. "You'll go batty when old man Moser's ghosts start prowling around."

The Morrisons and other people in the community had told him fearsome things about the Moser place. Scary tales about noises and inexplicable sights. Moser, an irascible old man of the woods, had died twenty years before, and his bones lay buried in an unmarked grave somewhere near the cabin. Since then, the unused one-room dwelling had crumbled into almost nothing, and it had taken Thad many days of labor to fortify it against the onslaughts of winter. One of his biggest jobs had been lugging a wagonload of green lumber, which had cost him a week's wages, up the hill and flooring as much of the shack as the boards would cover.

With the boldness and ambition of a twenty-year-old, Thad had gone into the woods. He ran his traps by day and spent the nights trying to keep warm in his crude bed on the floor near the fireplace. Many of the stones in the walls and top of the fireplace had sagged out of place, which made them look like rows of teeth ready to snap and gobble him up.

The first time he noticed anything unnatural about the fire was late one winter night when he woke up and saw the flames acting strangely. The fire had died to a bed of coals in front of the backlog, as usual. Thad raised his head and watched in fascination. He was lying on the floor with his feet stretched toward the mouth of the fireplace.

He saw an orange finger of flame curl up out of the bed of coals and then dance around in the air before it lashed swiftly toward his feet. Instinctively, he jerked his feet up under the blankets toward his body. He heard and felt something strike hard amid the ends of the blankets on the floor, where his feet had been only seconds before.

Twisting into a sitting position, he watched the long, menacing arm of flame sweep from side to side like a giant cobra searching for him. Occasionally the end of it fell swiftly, and he heard a thud as something struck the floor with force.

He got up, lit the candle on his table, moved to a far corner of the room, and wrapped the blankets around him. Soon the flashing flames slid back into the bed of coals. It became frightfully cold there in the corner on the half-frozen dirt floor. Too cold. The dying fire looked quite peaceful again. Thad moved his blankets back onto the floor in front of the fireplace and lay down. Warmer now, he dozed off.

Flashing light woke him. Long, jagged arms of flame were leaping out over him again. Quickly he rolled away from the fireplace, and as he looked back, the flames struck downward, and thuds sounded on the floor. Soon the flames receded again.

This time he shoved his slab table against the wall and, huddling in his blankets on the table, slept fitfully until dawn. Then he got up, threw kindling on the fire, and soon had a crackling blaze roaring up the chimney. Suddenly he saw it. There on the rough oak boards in front of the hearthstone were long, inch-deep imprints such as an axe or hatchet might have made. The wood around them was charred. He bent and examined the gashes closely, and his face clouded with disbelief as he recalled the experiences of the night before.

He finished with his traps early that day, walked the long trail down to the village of Tuckertown, and told the folks there about his experiences with the fire.

"Ahhh," they said. " 'Twas like we expected. You can't stay up there alone, boy. Old man Moser's ha'nts are after you. Everybody knows that place is jinxed."

But since no one offered him an alternative, the defiant young man turned back to the foreboding mountain, determined to stay out the winter in the Moser cabin, dancing fire or no.

On his way out of the village, he stopped by the clapboard home of Mary Ann, a girl of about his own age whom he had talked to a few times before. Her face blossomed into a smile like a crimson rose when she saw him. Brown hair rustled around her shoulders. Her hands untied the apron from her waist and smoothed her fresh gingham dress. Behind her, Thad saw her father come to the door and lean against it, regarding Thad with an expression of disdain saved for suitors with no means and little prospects.

An arm's length away, Thad spoke to the girl. "I'm going back up the mountain," he said awkwardly, with a sudden surge of inferiority and self-consciousness. "I won't be back till spring. I . . . I just thought I'd stop by and tell you I'd be back then."

She nodded. "I'm glad you did stop. I dread for you to spend the winter off up there in those terrible woods." Impulsively she unfastened the chain of a little golden locket from around her neck, pressed it into his hands, and stepped back. "Take this with you and bring it back to me in the spring."

"Mary Ann," came a rough masculine voice from the doorway, "you come on in the house."

Thad turned and waved to her once before he walked out of the yard and into the trees. The bleak December sky loosened a flurry of snowflakes as he hurried up the trail in the waning light of late afternoon.

It snowed that night and most of the next day.

Confined to the cabin, Thad kept the fireplace piled with logs, and the fire roared merrily up the chimney. During the night he made a discovery about the fire. As long as there was plenty of fuel on the fire, there was no sign of anything menacing or abnormal. But if he let it die down low, he could count on those long curling flames to rise and dance and flick out wildly and chop at the floor with an unseen tool. Mostly it occurred at night. But once Thad returned from his traps at high noon and heard hammering on the hearth boards.

Thad had a visitor a few days later, Bert Morrison, one of the boys he had worked with during the summer. Bert had heard from the villagers about the strange behavior of the fire, and he had come to see it firsthand.

"I gotta see it myself, Thad," Bert said, "before I'll believe it. I think you've been here alone so long you're seein' things that ain't there a-tall."

After a skimpy supper, the boys sat by the roaring fire and whittled and talked. Thad told Bert that, if anything should happen to him here during the winter, his belongings were to go to Mary Ann.

The warm fire lulled Bert into drowsiness, and he said that he was ready for bed. Thad spread some ragged blankets over the boards in front of the hearth, and Bert removed his heavy boots and lay down. The fire died slowly, and the light in the room grew dimmer. Pulling the blankets around him, Thad crawled on top of the table to watch and wait.

Some little time passed before Thad saw any movement in the fire. Bert snored soundly. Then the peaceful fire began its savage dance, the flames licking out viciously. Abruptly, the flames darted out into the room over Bert's body. Thad moved hurriedly to wake the boy and drag him out of danger.

But Bert's head lifted. Then he sat bolt upright, drawing up his feet. Just in time, too. The ends of the flames fell swiftly again and again. There were thuds muffled by the blankets where Bert's feet and legs had been an instant before.

For a moment, Bert sat there fascinated, a foolish look on his face, watching the wicked flames lash out over him. Thad lunged forward to drag him away. But Bert let out a terrified shriek, jumped up, and ran for the door, forgetting his boots. With a look of stark horror on his face, he was out the door before Thad could stop him.

Thad rushed to the door to look and listen. Outside, the snow lay in scattered patches under a brittle moon. A frigid wind cavorted among the tall pines and tore around the eaves of the cabin. Thad could hear Bert's wild shrieking far down the trail. There was no point in going after him. Bert knew the trail, and he wouldn't stop until he reached the village. As long as he kept running, he wouldn't freeze.

The winter passed slowly with its snow and ice and bitter cold. Oldsters reckoned it was one of the foulest winters seen in a lifetime.

It was well into the dark nights of March before the villagers began wondering when Thad would be coming down from the mountain with his winter's catch. After two consecutive afternoons of discussing it around the pot-bellied stove in the Tuckertown store, some of the younger men decided to pay Thad a neighborly visit. Maybe they could help him lug down his hides.

In the group that trudged up the mountain the next day was a grim-faced Bert Morrison. No smoke came from the old cabin as the men approached. The place looked dead. The rickety door had swelled and had to be forced open.

All the half-dozen men had filed inside the dim room before they saw it. The silence was complete, a stunned hush as the men stared with unbelieving eyes.

Scattered like scraps of rags and bark on the floor in front of the dead fireplace lay the barely recognizable pieces of a human body. It had been horribly hacked and mangled to bits.

The men backed outside, sick from the sight within the cabin. They wagged their heads and stared blankly at each other.

"Let's get away from this devilish place," one man said, retching dryly. "There ain't even enough left of him to bury decent."

But Bert Morrison remembered his promise. He kept his eyes averted as he ransacked the cabin for the personal effects of his deceased friend. He dumped them into a burlap sack he found hanging from a rafter pole. Included in the sack was a little golden locket on a tiny chain.

Tuckertown was a stricken and burdened community after the news circulated late that afternoon. A tense and sad-faced young woman shed tears as she looked through the scant belongings of the young man she had hoped someday to marry.

One of the men who had visited the cabin and witnessed the gruesome sight added a final touch of horror to the story.

"I saw it plain," he told the people. "That thing in the fireplace. The fire looked dead out, like it had been out for weeks. It weren't. Not plumb out. There was one lone red firecoal glowing in the ashes on one side. I saw it plain. It looked like a mean, evil red eye, glaring at you from straight outta Hell itself!"

That fire is not dead, even to this day, the old folks in the Yadkin River hill country will tell you. Sometimes, when it is late at night, and the fire in the fireplace has begun to burn low, and there seems to be only a single coal glowing red in the darkness, an old housewife will jump up quickly and put more wood on the fire, lest a single flame curl up from the ashes, waver in the air a moment, and then chop at you with hatchets of fire.

Sea-born Woman

from *The Flaming Ship of Ocracoke & Other Tales of the Outer Banks*
by Charles Harry Whedbee

The year was 1720, and the month was the often stormy September. The Irish emigrant ship, *Celestial Harp*, had made heavy weather of the voyage since leaving Belfast several weeks before. Head winds and stormy seas had made the trip a succession of miserable days and restbroken nights for the poor emigrants huddled below decks. The stench from the whale-oil lamps swinging from the low ceiling mixed with the human odors inevitable in such close confinement. The sickening roll and pitch of the ship distressed many an already queasy stomach, and the pitiful passengers were a sorry-looking lot indeed.

Most of them had worked long and hard, had scrimped and saved to accumulate passage money for this trip. Conditions were almost intolerably hard for the poor in Ireland at that time, and the dream of a life in that New World across the sea seemed, to many, like the hope of a Promised Land, a land of opportunity and of beginning again. This was the dream that sustained them. This was the vision that, even now, was stronger than the fear of sudden shipwreck and death in the stormy North Atlantic.

John and Mary O'Hagan considered themselves to be more fortunate than most of the emigrants. John had his skill in carpentry, which was sure to be much in demand in the new country, and Mary had the frugality and good common sense of the typical Irish housewife. More than that, Mary was expecting the birth of their first child any day now, and, thank God, there were two midwives in the company, thus assuring her the very best of care. The O'Hagans considered themselves to be greatly blessed.

Two days earlier the weather had cleared, and, as if an omen of brighter days to come, the wind had abated and hauled favorably and the seas had subsided. At long last, the emigrants were able to come out on deck and enjoy the sights, sounds, and fresh smells of a brisk day at sea. Their joy was complete when the captain told them that the worst weather was now past and that they were almost within sight of Massachusetts Colony, where they could expect to land within the week.

Just over the horizon, some twenty or thirty miles to the southward, another group of seafarers was also rejoicing over the improvement in the weather. The flotilla of five pirate ships under the command of the famous buccaneer captain, Edward Low, had had very poor hunting, and the motley crews were eager and fretting for action. Discipline had become more of a problem than ever among the cutthroat sailors, and there had even been rumblings of a possible mutiny and a departure to warmer climes and better hunting grounds.

The pirates had come north hoping to intercept merchant ships loaded with valuable cargoes but, so far, had encountered only the huge, crashing, green seas of the North Atlantic. The gale-force winds had blown almost incessantly, and never a potential quarry had come into view, although many could have slipped past undetected in the driving rain and mist. The sudden break in the weather and the reappearance of the sun brightened the spirits of the sea rovers, and they were literally spoiling for action.

This mission had been undertaken jointly by the five ships, so when the weather improved, Captain Low called a hurried conference of his captains on the afterdeck of his ship. There it was decided that three of the five vessels would sail in various southerly directions in search of prey. Low's ship and the *Delight*, captained by Low's favorite subordinate, Francis Carrington Spriggs, would sail in still other directions towards the north. Rendezvous was set for six months later at New Providence, which at that time served as one of the major pirate capitals of the world.

Just before first light the next morning, Spriggs and his crew of eighteen weighed anchor on the *Delight*, eased the ship away from Low's ship, and made full sail northward in the darkness. As the *Delight* squared away on her new course and left the other ships behind, Captain Spriggs himself raised his new flag swiftly to the main truck, the highest point on the vessel. The crew cheered lustily at the sight of this sinister symbol of piracy, and several broke into a clumsy sort of hornpipe dance. The young captain had designed the flag to suit his own particular taste, and it was unique in the pirate world. It consisted of a large rectangular piece of black cloth on which was sewn the figure of a white skeleton holding an hourglass in one bony hand and an arrow on which was impaled a bleeding heart in the other hand. The flag snapped in the fresh, early morning breeze as though it had a life of its own.

Northward then drove the *Delight* and her newly independent captain. A fresh breeze poured over her port quarter, and her damp sails were set and drawing well. Northward she sped and, as fate would have it, on a course which would intercept that of the plodding *Celestial Harp* and her human cargo.

It was about first light the next morning when the lookout in the main shrouds of the pirate ship cried his sighting of the emigrant vessel. By midday the two ships lay alongside each other and the brief resistance on the part of the crew of the *Celestial Harp* had ended. The shipload of pitiful passengers were now all pirate captives and in very real danger of immediate and violent death.

Captain Spriggs' disappointment at the poverty of his prize can be imagined. The captured ship, herself, was too slow and clumsy to be worth confiscating, and the few supplies she had left were hardly worth transferring to his own craft. The anger of the pirate skipper was an evil token for his captives. Even for one so young, Captain Spriggs was already building a reputation, not only for bravery, but for cruelty, for it was his habit to put to death all captured seamen so that they might not later testify against him. "Dead men tell no tales," he had cried on more than one occasion such as this, and he was prepared to practice his philosophy now.

Maybe it was because of his disappointment or maybe it was just to impress his crew that he now devised a new and more dramatic way to forever close the mouths of his captives. Pirate crews were always notoriously close to mutiny, and an example of savagery was usually helpful in keeping them in their place. Whatever the reason, the method of extermination, this time, was to be most unusual.

Personally supervising his crew, Spriggs ordered kegs of gunpowder secured at strategic places near the waterline of the emigrant ship. Fuses of varying lengths were then run from these powder kegs to a central spot on the deck. According to the pirate's calculations, if he lighted the fuses at one-minute intervals, he would have time to get off the doomed ship and, then, all the powder kegs would explode simultaneously, blowing the ship to bits. The men of the *Celestial Harp*, passengers and crew alike, were chained to masts and stanchions so that they could neither interfere with the grand explosion nor leap into the sea to save themselves. The careful planning and preparation was all accomplished before the terrified eyes of the chained men, whose pleading and prayers the pirates scornfully ignored. This was to be a blast that would live in pirate history.

Meanwhile, below the foredeck and completely unknown to the pirates, another drama was taking place. The two midwives, working in frantic haste, were preparing for the birth of Mary O'Hagan's child. Whether or not the excitement and despair caused by the pirate invasion had hastened the event, there was now no time to consider, nor did it matter. The greatest of God's recurring miracles was about to take place, and the three women most immediately concerned would not be bothered with what was going on above decks, even though death itself might be imminent. A baby was about to be born.

Thus was Mary O'Hagan delivered of a beautiful, large baby girl in the dim light of swinging oil lamps in the stuffy hold of a ship which was hove to and rolling restlessly in the waves. A delighted smile creased the face of the elder midwife as she held the new-born child up by the ankles and slapped her smartly with an open hand across the little buttocks. The sound of the first healthy wail from the baby's lungs echoed and reechoed in the confines of the hold, penetrated the hatch openings, and sounded on the deck of the *Celestial Harp*, where men stood ready to torture and kill upon their leader's signal.

What prompted Captain Francis Spriggs' next move is known only to God. It could have been that he felt some stirring of pity for his helpless victims after his first anger at their poverty had passed. It could have been that he suddenly remembered an ancient superstition of pirates that it is very lucky for a new captain to release his first prize, just as some fishermen always throw back the first fish caught. It is quite possible that he quickly realized that the blessed event provided him with a means of saving face before his crew, while making his offering on the altar of luck at the same time. Whatever the reason, he reacted immediately.

Beaming with honest joy when he was told of the birth, he sent below to inquire if the new-born baby was a boy or a girl. Upon learning that the child was a girl, he fairly capered with delight. He pointed again and again, first to the name board of his own ship where the title *Delight* appeared in foot-high gilt letters, then back to the hatchway from whence came the lusty cries of the baby. He seemed to sense some connection between the ship's name and the arrival of the child, and the coincidence pleased him beyond measure.

Summoning the master of the emigrant ship, the first mate, and the baby's father John O'Hagan, the pirate chieftain made them a proposition. "Only name the baby girl for my dear old mother," he said, "and I'll let your ship go free. Call her Jerushia—Jerushia Spriggs O'Hagan—and you can all go with my blessing."

Well, it didn't take them long to accept such a one-sided choice as that, and so the bargain was made. The gunpowder kegs and unlit fuses were removed from the *Celestial Harp* as the baby's name was entered in the ship's log as Jerushia Spriggs O'Hagan. Both John and Mary O'Hagan signed the book in agreement to the name, and it was duly witnessed by both midwives, the captain, and the first mate.

So pleased was Captain Spriggs with the acceptance of his offer that he immediately sent a small boat back to the *Delight* to fetch a bolt of cloth-of-gold, which he gave to Mary O'Hagan with the strict admonition that it be used only to make a wedding gown for Jerushia when she was grown to womanhood and had chosen her man.

On this note, the two ships parted. The *Celestial Harp* plowed, once again, on her way to Massachusetts, and the *Delight* headed southward, her cannon booming out a long, rolling salute of twelve guns as the distance widened between the vessels.

In the New World, John O'Hagan's skills with the drawing knife, the saw, and the chisel stood him in good stead. Settling in New Bedford, he developed into one of the finest shipbuilders available, and his services were much in demand. As he worked and prospered, little Jerushia grew and developed until the fame of her Irish beauty spread far and wide. The sea baby had become beautiful on a majestic scale. A full six feet tall she was, slender and graceful. To set off her willowy figure, she was blessed with hair the color of mahogany, which fell like a cape to her waist. With lovely, regular features and an open, sunny disposition, she was the favorite of young and old. Only one incident marred those golden years. When she was twelve, Jerushia's mother died, and the duties of the household fell on her young shoulders.

All during those happy years, there was never a Christmas which passed without a very special gift from Captain Spriggs, and, on each birthday, he sent her a bolt of very fine cloth of some description from which she delighted in making her own special dresses. The pirate had searched out the whereabouts of the girl he had spared and took pleasure in remembering her special days. Jerushia called him "Godfather," although she actually saw him only a very few times during those years.

In due time, she chose from among her many suitors a young sea captain. She was married in New Bedford, in a dress of Captain Spriggs' cloth-of-gold. The union was blessed with three children, all boys. It was, indeed, a happy period in Jerushia's life, a time of loving and sharing, of growth and blessed contentment.

What happened to Captain Francis Spriggs for several years after that September day in 1720, when he sailed away from the reprieved *Celestial Harp*, is not clear. It is almost certain that he did sail back to the pirate rendezvous at New Providence, for if he had not, his fellow pirates would have hunted him down and murdered him for breaking faith with the Brotherhood of the Sea, as they called themselves. Apparently, his career as a pirate did not last very long, however. According to British Navy records, he met his first, and only, defeat fairly soon after the *Celestial Harp* incident. While plundering the Bay of Honduras, Spriggs and his crew were surprised by a British war ship. The *Delight* was run aground, and Spriggs and his ruffians escaped to shore.

There are no more official accounts of his pirating and, so far as the records of the British Admiralty show, he just dropped out of sight. There is no evidence that he ever took the King's Pardon, as so many of the Brotherhood who wanted to come ashore and live as honest men did. Neither is there any record that he thereafter engaged in any unlawful activity. His faithful remembering of Jerushia's birthdays and Christmases provides the only record of him for many years.

But, in 1741, Spriggs again surfaced on the sea of history as we catch a glimpse of him in Yorktown, Virginia. Here he was a ship owner and merchant of considerable means, owning several vessels engaged in trade with foreign countries. There is a record of his business and an account of his marriage and the death of his bride in less than a year in one of the terrible epidemics of those times. Still later it is known that he moved to

Beaufort Town, sometimes called Hongry Town in that era, for a few years.

Meanwhile, the shadow of tragedy had fallen on Jerushia. Her father was killed in a shipyard accident, and, in a terrible storm in 1758, her husband and her youngest son were lost at sea. Her oldest son had become a preacher and went to live as a missionary among the Indians of the western plains. Her second son took over a portion of his father's business, but he married a woman as different from his mother as can be imagined. There always seemed to be some difference, some misunderstanding, between the two women, and Jerushia, while adequately provided for, lived a very lonely life. There was not much a widow could do in New Bedford in those days and, to make things worse, the business began to suffer reverses. Soon Jerushia was reduced to very modest circumstances and, at times, she felt the pinch of actual want.

This was the atmosphere when, in September of that year, her birthday came around and, for the very first time, no delivery van brought the customary bolt of cloth to her door. Already depressed, she broke down and cried miserably. Later that afternoon, she answered the bell at her door and saw, standing before her, a figure that was at once familiar and unfamiliar.

Her caller was a tall, erect man in his early sixties with graying hair and deeply tanned, but young-looking, skin. Some little thing, some mannerism of his as he removed his hat with a flourish and smiled at her, served to trigger her memory. With a rush of happiness, she recognized "Godfather Spriggs" and, like a little girl, threw her arms around his neck in welcome.

What a time those two must have had reminiscing on that day! The bolt of cloth was not missing; Francis Spriggs had brought it with him. He was in New Bedford on business, he told her, and must leave within the week. She told him of her loneliness, and he called on the young woman daily while he was there, telling her of his plans and his problems.

Having accumulated a great deal of wealth, he planned to retire from the world of business, for he wanted nothing more from life than to spend his remaining years somewhere near the sea, where he could read and perhaps tend a little garden and listen to the talk of seafaring men. He had purchased a plot of ground in a North Carolina town called Portsmouth, which was just south of Ocracoke Inlet and just across that inlet from Pilot Town, as some people called the village of Ocracoke. The Colony of Carolina was developing this town, and it was to be the biggest seaport anywhere around, with wharves and warehouses and shipfitting basins. There were many stores and shops and even plans for a large hospital to be located there. He had bought his plot at a reasonable price from his old friend, Colonel Michael Coutanch of Bath Town, and was even now building a two-story house with all the most modern conveniences known to the building trade.

Knowing Jerushia's loneliness, he asked her to move to Portsmouth as his housekeeper. In return, he offered her an excellent salary, considerate treatment, and the promise of the house itself at his death. Jerushia accepted the offer gladly, and thus began another of the happiest periods of her life.

Housekeeper she was, indeed, but Captain Spriggs, from the very first, treated her more like a daughter than a servant. Old enough to be her father and without children of his own, he lavished on her all the comforts he would have given to his own children. Jerushia had to plan the meals and buy provisions in the village of Portsmouth, but Spriggs provided her with a cook and a maid to do the heavy cleaning. Knowing her love of horses, he bought her a matched pair of black Arabians and a shiny black buggy to ride in. What a beautiful sight it must have been to see this tall, lovely woman, dressed all in widow's black but with a wealth of dark red hair streaming out behind her, as she drove her horses at full speed down the one road that extended the length of Portsmouth Island or walked them into Portsmouth Town to shop for groceries.

As Captain Spriggs had promised, "Spriggs' Luck," as the house was called, had all the conveniences known in that day. The ground floor was comprised of a large parlor and an equally large dining room. Off to one side was a sitting room and, on the other, a combination library-office, where the captain handled the details of the shipping business in which he was still engaged. It was here that he also entertained his infrequent business visitors.

The second story contained four large bedrooms, and, out back, a dogtrot (now called a breezeway) connected the house with the kitchen and pantry, which were built separate from the main structure in order to protect the main house from the hazard of fire and the odors of cooking. The "necessary house" was a rather commodius two-room structure built some fifty or sixty feet to the rear of the kitchen and reached via a roofed, brick walkway extending from the back door of the kitchen. Thus it was entirely possible to walk, during a pouring rainstorm, from the main house through the dogtrot and the kitchen to the necessary house without once feeling a drop of rain or setting foot on the bare ground.

Spriggs' Luck had one macabre feature. In the large parlor there was a huge fireplace, complete with andirons and an iron cooking hook. The hearthstone in front of this opening was a large slab of solid marble some six inches thick, which served also as the lid for a concrete burial vault located immediately underneath. It was Spriggs' fancy that he wanted to be buried here so that his body would always be above the reach of the storm tides and still be part and parcel of the house that he loved so well. He had seen what those storms could, and sometimes would, do to an ordinary graveyard, and the thought haunted him. He made Jerushia promise that, should she outlive him, she would see that his burial was exactly as he wanted it.

Located well to the rear of the building was a small peach orchard with fifteen or twenty peach trees and a small pergola, or summerhouse, nestled in the center. Here the housekeeper could while away the afternoon hours of a spring day at reading or making lace, with the scent of the many bay trees and the peach blossoms heavy in the air and the muted sound of the surf in the middle distance. Off to one side were the carriage house and the stables where her blooded horses were kept.

Jerushia was far from selfish in her happiness. As though sensing in some way that she could not keep good fortune unless she shared it with the less happy, she became a veritable angel of mercy to the womenfolk of Portsmouth Town and Portsmouth Island. She trained herself to become as skillful as any midwife at the many duties surrounding childbirth, and her warm sympathy and ready wit made her a welcome assistant in times of stress and trouble. On her frequent trips by boat to New Berne and Beaufort and Edenton, she always inquired ahead of time what her neighbors would like brought to them. If she had to add a coin or two from her own purse to make up an unexpectedly high purchase price, no one was ever the wiser.

The unusual circumstances surrounding her birth soon became known to the island women, and, with the mysticism that comes so naturally to coastland folk, she became known simply as Sea-born Woman. As time passed, the people of Portsmouth grew to love her and rely on her and trust her.

So far as Jerushia knew, her benefactor did not have an enemy in world. The days of his piratical beginnings were long past and almost never mentioned. The days flowed by like a lazy stream, and Captain Spriggs seemed happy to live in Spriggs' Luck, taking part in an occasional fishing of the gill nets with friends from the village or conferring with an occasional visitor about some business manner. There were long, sunlit days in summer, too, when the Captain and his housekeeper would stroll the ocean beach of Portsmouth Island for miles. They would watch the many ships that used the port and wonder whence they came and whither they were bound.

Enemies he must have had, however, and they eventually searched him out and found him. Returning from the village late one afternoon in the winter of 1770, Jerushia wheeled her horses into the wide circle she usually described before entering the stables. As she approached the stable yard, both horses reared and shied in fright, so that it required all her strength to control them. In the fading light of the setting sun she saw, to her horror, what had frightened them. There on the sand lay Captain Spriggs, face down, with a dirk driven to the hilt between his shoulder blades. He was quite dead.

The footprints that must have marked the sandy soil had all been carefully erased with a branch broken from one of the peach trees. Near the body lay half of a sheet of parchment, and, in the center of that parchment, a black spot about the size of a shilling had been laboriously inscribed with a quill and black ink. The pirate mark of revenge-death!

All efforts to find the killer or killers proved futile. There were no strangers in town other than the usual polyglot assortment of sailors on leave from the many ships that lay at anchor in the harbor. There was no way to or from the island except by boat; nevertheless, it was impossible to find even one logical suspect.

As the old pirate had wished, Sea-born Woman buried him in the vault he had prepared. Sailors and local fisherman rigged a block and tackle to hoist the marble hearthstone so that the body could be lowered into the vault. Then the marble was cemented back into place to make an airtight seal. And, true to his word, Spriggs had left a will in his own handwriting, bequeathing Spriggs' Luck and all the surrounding grounds to Jerushia.

From that moment on, Jerushia lived not only in that house, but largely for that house. Always a good housekeeper, she now made a fetish of keeping Spriggs' Luck in immaculate condition. Never a speck of dust was allowed to accumulate on the fine furniture. In the spring and summer, she placed fresh flowers in the fireplace opening just alongside the marble hearthstone. Often passersby at night would see her lonely figure seated in a chair in front of the hearth, a whale-oil lamp burning brightly on a table by her side.

When the American Revolution flared into full hostilities, Ocracoke Inlet and Portsmouth Harbor became two of the focal points of combat. The deep-water channel through Ocracoke Inlet was then, as it is now, a twisting, hazardous, and ever-changing thing. Raiding British warships had to be of shallow draft to negotiate that channel, and, once inside the bar, they found American galleys, manned by patriots at the long oar sweeps, awaiting them. Resembling ancient Roman slave galleys, these oar-driven vessels were very swift and maneuverable and were usually more than a match for the slower Britishers. Thus, Portsmouth and Ocracoke harbors, as well as the Town of Portsmouth, often rang with the sound of naval gunfire, as miniature naval engagements were fought to the death in those sheltered waters.

Raiding parties of British Marines were often put ashore to forage and to burn the countryside and kill all the livestock they could find. These invading forces were met by small groups of militia formed by the native fisherman. Usually the advantage lay with the islanders. They knew the terrain and were perfectly at home in that environment of sand and wind and roaring surf. The British had the better weapons, though, and the advantage of professional training as soldiers with the discipline of regulars. In spite of this, no actual occupation of Portsmouth Town was ever achieved by the British, although they kept considerable pressure on the thin defensive forces stationed there.

For the five or six years the fighting actually lasted on the Outer Banks, Jerushia was a tower of strength to her people. She converted Spriggs' Luck into a very efficient hospital and recruited and trained several of the local ladies as nurses. Reading avidly such medical books as she could find, she did her best to relieve, mend, and cure the casualties brought to her beloved home. The islanders had always been fond of her. Now, they began to regard her as a special saint who had been sent especially for their healing and comfort. They tipped their hats or pulled at their forelocks in gestures of respect and admiration when the tall, graceful figure, dressed always in black, walked by. They relied on her, and she never failed them as long as she lived. She was the living spirit of Portsmouth Town for many, many years, and she helped them to persevere until the Revolution was won.

Sea-born Woman died in her sleep one peaceful spring night in 1810 at the ripe old age of ninety. She was tenderly and lovingly laid to rest in the little yaupon grove to the rear of Spriggs' Luck by her friends and neighbors. There had been no illness, no suffering, no long period of disability. It is said that she just stopped living very quietly and easily.

But if the natives thought that they had seen the last of this remarkable woman when they buried her, they were mistaken. Some three years later the first recorded appearance of what is said to be her ghost took place.

During the War of 1812, when the British came so close to retaking their former American colonies, the first manifestation occurred. In 1813, the King's forces landed on Portsmouth Island and began the systematic slaughter of all the livestock they could find in order, they claimed, to procure fresh meat for their ships lying offshore. Houses were ransacked and looted, and many islanders were robbed of their few valuable possessions. It was inevitable that a fine structure like Spriggs' Luck, now boarded up and tightly shuttered, should be the object of such an attack.

An English foraging party made the mistake of breaking into the splendid old mansion one night on one of their raids. They ran into an experience none of them ever forgot. No sooner had they forced the front door and entered, torches held high for illumination, than they were set upon by a whirling creature with a mane of flowing, red hair who was dressed in a long black gown.

The apparition laid about her with an oar and soon had the British in utter confusion. As if blown by some tremendous gust of wind, all the torches were extinguished in the same instant. The terrified sailors began to strike out blindly with their knives, seriously wounding several of their company. When they finally did fumble their way to the door, they beat a hasty retreat, carrying their wounded with them. Back on shipboard, they spread the word of their eerie experience, and never again was a foraging party to visit Spriggs' Luck.

Following the war, the fine old home was sold and resold many times, sometimes to people who were delighted with their purchase and sometimes to others who were terrified and wanted to get rid of it as quickly as possible. The difference was Jerushia. If she found the new owners to be lazy and inefficient housekeepers who let her home become run down and dilapidated, she would make life miserable for them with appearances and manifestations and sleepless nights until she finally drove them away.

If, on the other hand, she saw that the owners took good care of Spriggs' Luck and kept it in a good state of repair, she would give them no trouble whatsoever. She had loved that house during her life, and she was not about to desert it now to unappreciative tenants.

Not only did she love and protect her former home; she also continued her interest in the islanders. Many are the tales of her help given to poor fishermen in their time of danger or of need. Often a wife in childbirth was comforted and soothed by the presence of that six-foot feminine figure with the shock of red hair. Her people did not and they do not fear her. They believe in her and respect and love her to this day for the aid and comfort she has brought a hardy, but often underprivileged, people.

For generations Spriggs' Luck stood as an inspiration and historic landmark in Portsmouth Town, but in time its luck ran out and it met the fate of all man-made structures on these Outer Banks.

It was the big hurricane, then called an equinoctial storm, of 1899 that destroyed most of what sea-born Jerushia had fought so long and so well to preserve. All during that historic storm, according to established folk memory, the natives heard wild cries of despair as the raging winds ripped and tore at the structure. The screams and the howling of the wind reached an awful crescendo at the same instant. At that second, Spriggs' Luck collapsed with a mighty roar. Board was torn from board, and the wreckage was whipped and strewn across the entire width of the island. The wind-driven tide pounded against the foundations and scattered fragments of wreckage even farther inland.

It is hard to imagine the fury of such a wind gone insane. Facing into the wind, it is impossible to breathe, and if one puts his back to the blow, it seems as though one's very lungs will be sucked from his body by that awful pressure. Tiny straws are actually blown through the trunks of small trees, so awful is the force of the moving air. Strongly built houses just disappear as if they were made of cards, and the whole appearance of a region is drastically altered in the winking of an eye. Such a storm was the 1899 disaster.

When the blow had spent its fury and the winds and seas had once again subsided, all that was left of the ancient building was the stub of a brick chimney and the massive hearthstone, now at ground level, that marked the final resting place of the old pirate. And that is all that remains today of Spriggs' Luck, now called "Brigand's Luck" by some.

Sea-born Woman did not vanish with the structure, however. Full many a sailor has stood to the wheel of his boat trying to steer a safe course through fog or driving rain to enter Ocracoke Inlet and has suddenly become aware of a tall, willowy figure standing by his side, mahogany hair floating free in the wind and long arm and forefinger pointing the way to safe passage. Still the tall, graceful figure can be seen on rare occasions as she moves about that marble slab. Sometimes, they say, if you listen very carefully and remain very still, you can hear the faint sound of gay laughter and the music of long, long ago.

The Beckoning Hands

from *Outer Banks Mysteries and Seaside Stories*
by Charles Harry Whedbee

The basins of the Roanoke and Chowan Rivers were two of the earliest centers of civilization in the New World. Many beautiful homes were built along their shores, and towns such as Plymouth and Edenton played an important part in the settling of the Province of Carolina, both under the Lords Proprietors and under the royal governors.

Most of the mansions built along the lovely shorelines were the creations of planters and import merchants, but at least one was built at the direction of a famous pirate who wanted not only a secure place to keep his plunder, but also a comfortable and gracious showplace where his noble friends—governors and statesmen and such—could be entertained in the gracious style to which they were accustomed. After all, he considered himself a sort of import merchant, too. You see, even in those days it was not unusual for some of the more successful criminals to want to cross the line into respectability for themselves and their families.

The edifice of which we speak is still standing on the top of a small but high bluff overlooking the Chowan River. It was carefully planned down to the last cubic foot. Its masonry walls are very thick, almost like a fort, making it nearly soundproof and very easy to heat in winter and cool in summer. A large basement gives opening to a brick-lined tunnel that descends through the heart of the bluff to a well-concealed door at the level of the river.

This made the unloading of boats a very practical matter, as well as a very private one. No prying eye could possibly see what was being transferred from rowboats to the mouth of the tunnel or vice versa.

The high ground upon which the house is located afforded an excellent lookout both up and down the river, so the occupants had ample notice of the approach of any travelers by water and could take any steps they considered expedient. As most travel in those days was by boat, the beautiful home was indeed a very snug and secure nest.

At the will of the owner, the splendid structure could be either a fort or a gracious palace. It was built by the most skillful artisans and of only the very best materials obtainable from the seven seas of the world. In addition to the stones of which the basic structure was built, there were rosewood, mahogany, and teakwood from the tropics and golden oak from the timbers of captured ships. The house was built with all the meticulous attention to detail and strength that the skilled boatwright is accustomed to putting into the building of an ocean-going vessel. It is still sound and secure down to this very day.

Perhaps the most striking feature of the interior of the mansion was the grand entrance. Here a huge hall was lighted by sterling silver sconces bearing wax candles that blazed brilliantly. A very wide staircase opened just opposite the massive front doors. Made of highly polished mahogany, the staircase swept upward in a graceful flair and opened on an upstairs hall, which served as a passageway to the rooms of the upper floors. Carpeted with fabulous oriental rugs, the hall and stair gave dramatic welcome to the house as one entered the front doors. The rugs are no longer there, but that magnificent staircase still sweeps in its graceful and imposing curve, inviting the guest to enter and explore the regions above.

Large parlors and dining rooms open off this large entrance hall, and in its early days a kitchen was located to the rear of the house, providing easy and direct access to the dining room through a butler's pantry.

The only trouble was that the family of the would-be-respectable pirate would never live there with him.

His lovely young wife did not approve of his piratical ways nor of his affairs with other ladies of the area. But she was also apprehensive about a curse that had been laid on her pirate husband by an old hag who lived in Nags Head Woods.

It seems he had "pressed" or kidnapped the old woman's son, an only child, into service aboard the pirate ship. The boy had subsequently been killed during an attack upon a merchant ship, and the old crone blamed the pirate captain for depriving her of any hope of grandchildren. In spite of a rather large sum of money given to her by the buccaneer, she swore a curse on his head to the effect that he, too, should never know the joy of being a grandparent, but that his line should be cut off for all time and forever.

It was shortly after news of this malediction reached her that the brigand's wife left him and took their daughter back to her home town of Charleston, South Carolina. She maintained separate quarters in a lovely house there, and the pirate was free to visit her and their beautiful young daughter Caroline.

Several years later, the pirate captain caught a fever in the West Indies and died aboard ship. He was buried at sea according to the custom of the Brotherhood of the Sea, and his faithful first mate then sailed openly into Charleston harbor to carry the news of his passing to his widow. He also carried his captain's sword, other personal belongings, and the shipmaster's share of the accumulated loot, which amounted, in value, to a sizable sum. This, together with her other holdings and previous gifts from her husband, left the widow quite comfortably fixed.

Among the properties inherited by the widow and her daughter was the beautiful mansion overlooking the river, and the two of them soon took up residence there. It was much cooler in the summers, and the winters did not seem to be as piercingly cold or damp. The house was magnificently appointed and very comfortable, and the neighbors on adjoining plantations were what was termed "quality folk." All in all, it seemed a nearly ideal place to complete the rearing of a daughter.

Caroline grew in grace and in beauty and soon was the toast of the entire region. The great stone house often rang with music and merriment as the young folk of the province gathered for extended homeparties that lasted several days at the very least. Life was pleasant, unhurried, and serene. There was plenty of delicious food, plenty of good and genteel company, plenty of light and laughter, and above all, plenty of time in which to live the good life to the fullest.

Or so they thought.

Youth and laughter and friendship blossomed into love for the beautiful, diminutive Caroline, and wedding arrangements were soon made for her marriage to the scion of one of the oldest and wealthiest families in the entire Roanoke-Chowan area.

The wedding ceremony was to take place at the home of the bride, and invitations went out to all the great and many of the near-great in that whole region. It was to be a brilliant social affair, with the ceremony to be performed by a visiting bishop of the Anglican Church. The house was beautifully decorated with Christmas decorations, for the ceremony was to take place on New Year's Day, still a part of the Christmas season. A string orchestra was brought in from Edenton to furnish the wedding music, and the days preceding New Year's were an endless round of parties and holiday festivities.

The wedding day arrived at last. The bishop made an imposing figure in his vestments as he stood very erect, prayer book in hand, ready to perform the nuptial ceremony. He and all the other guests were assembled in the great hall. The nervous young bridegroom was in his place beside the bishop, and the bride was to enter from a dressing room located just off the great hall.

The orchestra struck up the wedding music, played it once, then again, but the bride did not appear. The bishop cleared his throat and glanced over at the mother of the bride, who was beginning to experience the first symptoms of panic. A chill of premonition gripped her, and she remembered the curse of the Nags Head hag.

Then, from above the level of their heads, came . . . a very feminine giggle!

All eyes snapped immediately to the head of the huge stairway, and there they beheld the bride in all her wedding finery, looking down at them with twinkling eyes and with a teasing smile on her pretty lips. She looked no bigger than a child as she stood there, radiantly happy and the most beautiful thing the bridegroom had ever seen. In spite of warnings that he must not look upon his bride in her wedding dress until she stood beside him at the altar, the young man could not take his eyes off her.

Tiny Caroline stood there for a brief moment, poised like a bird. She was reveling in the adoration and adulation flowing toward her from her beloved and her friends on the floor below.

Then, with an impish grin and looking directly into the eyes of her fiancé, she taunted, "Catch me and you may kiss me." She tossed her pretty, lace-bedecked head and beckoned to him with both her hands. Turning, she ran swiftly along the upstairs hall and disappeared around a corner.

Accepting the challenge, the young bridegroom leaped forward and ran up the broad stairway, three steps at a time, until he reached the hall above. Then he turned in the direction his beloved had taken and ran down the hallway after her.

There was no Caroline!

Up and down the halls he ran and into all the rooms, and still he could not find his bride. Calling her, he begged her to come out of her hiding place, as the wedding guests were becoming restless and the bishop was distinctly annoyed at this frivolous interruption of the religious ceremony.

Soon amusement or annoyance turned into genuine concern as the whole wedding party joined in the search for the missing girl. The great stone house was searched thoroughly, and the grounds around the house were carefully explored for hundreds of yards, but without producing a sign of the young girl. No strangers had been seen in the vicinity, and there was no known wild beast thereabouts that was large enough to have carried her off. No boats were missing from any of the piers along the waterfront.

Caroline had just disappeared without a trace.

After several months of futile search, Caroline's bereaved mother closed up the big stone house and moved away. It is said that the mysterious disappearance of her lovely daughter continued to grieve her and stayed on her mind so much that she soon became deranged and would talk of nothing but her lost bride-girl. There is no doubt that her grief shortened her life. The poor, troubled lady died without ever finding out what had become of Caroline.

The very next New Year's night, one year to the day after the strange disappearance, some children in the neighborhood of the great stone house came home badly frightened and told their parents of seeing a ghostly, white face floating and flitting from window to window inside the closed mansion. They said the "thing" beckoned enticingly with two ghostly, white hands. Their frightened parents forbade them to go ever again upon the grounds of the old pirate's mansion. Of course, being children, they did go back, but none of them was ever harmed.

Year after year, always on New Year's night, the pallid face and beckoning hands continued to appear in the windows of the house until the ghost became a local and then a regional attraction. Many brave people tried to solve the mystery of the apparition, but when they gained admittance to the house, the phenomenon always vanished with a long and pitiful sigh.

The old pirate's beautiful home became known as "the house with the beckoning hands," and prudent people avoided it whenever they could. Nevertheless, many upright and reliable people—people of unquestioned sobriety—swore that they continued to see those beckoning hands and that pitiful face, but no one could solve the mystery.

Then, years later, a man who had made a deep study of such things rented the house from its owners to try to get to the bottom of the strange occurrence. Many believed he was a little touched in the head to be searching for a solution to a mystery that had gone unexplained all those years.

He actually moved into the house to try to obtain, firsthand, the feeling and the mood of the place. All by himself, he searched the house from top to bottom again and again. He never actually saw the beckoning hands or the wistful face, but he was convinced that his neighbors were telling the truth.

Then, on New Year's night, after he had waited in vain for the apparition, he fell asleep in the huge feather bed in the master bedroom of the house. As he slept he dreamed a very vivid dream.

He dreamed that he was witnessing that strange, interrupted wedding ceremony of many years before. He saw all the actors in the event as though from a vantage point above and beyond the wedding party, so he could see all of them at one time.

In his dream he saw the bridegroom leaping up the stairs in pursuit of his young, lovely bride, and he saw tiny Caroline turn and run down the hall in mock fright from her beloved.

And then he saw it. As Caroline dashed along the hall and turned a corner, she lost her balance in her long wedding dress and fell against the wall for support. Her steadying hand reached into a secret crevice in that stone wall and touched a secret lever. He saw a trapdoor open beneath her feet, and he caught a flash of wedding finery as she fell through that trapdoor and into a secret, windowless room beneath. He saw the trapdoor reclose as the heavy stone flooring turned upon its metal pivot and glided into place, locking shut with a metallic click.

In his dream, Caroline was entombed alive! The sheer horror of his vivid dream shocked him into consciousness, and he awoke with a scream.

Did his ears betray him or did he hear the high-pitched cackle of an old hag? As he rolled from his bed, the first light of a winter dawn was breaking over the eastern sky.

Without more ado, but trembling as if he had an ague, our researcher went directly to that portion of the hall he had seen so clearly in his dream. The stone wall was still there, and so was that secret crack or joint between the stones. Pushing his hand wrist-deep into the aperture, he felt the end of a rusty metal lever which, with great exertion, he was able to move.

Slowly, slowly, and with a great groaning sound as though it were reluctant to reveal its secret, the huge stone in the floor began to swing on its now rusty pivot until it stood fully open. A vagrant beam of sunlight fell directly into the opening before him.

There, on the floor of that secret room, he beheld a tiny human skeleton, almost as small as a child's, the bones of both hands extended along the floor in a beckoning gesture. On the head of the skeleton there was a trace of ancient white lace, almost like snow upon its brow. The wedding veil of lovely Caroline.

And thus was the mystery finally solved. The remains of poor Caroline were given Christian burial, and the treacherous trapdoor was sealed shut so that it could never again imprison an unsuspecting traveler along that hallway.

The beckoning hands?

Well, most of the people in the neighborhood will tell you that they disappeared from that day on, but there are others who will tell you that they can still be seen, but only on a dark New Year's night. They are beckoning, ever beckoning.

The Ghost Who Rang the Gatehouse Bell

from *Tales of the South Carolina Low Country*
by Nancy Rhyne

Ole Dan Tucker was a funny old man,
He washed his face in a frying pan,
He combed his hair with a wagon wheel
and died with a toothache in his heel.

The Dan Tucker immortalized in this folk song was the second governor of the Bermudas, and it was from Bermuda that a Daniel Tucker came to Litchfield Plantation in the late 1700s. Descendants of that Daniel Tucker owned the plantation, three miles west of Pawleys Island, until 1904.

There was no more remarkable family in the South Carolina Low Country than the Tuckers. Each generation was borne along on prosperity, and the gifts of fortune were lavished on them from the cradle to the grave.

The mansion stood in a grove of gnarled oak trees at the end of a deeply shadowed avenue of moss-draped oaks when the Tuckers took ownership of the property in the eighteenth century. Dan Tucker was a politician, and his plantation became well known during his years of ownership. When he died in 1797, he left Litchfield to three sons: John Hyrne, Daniel, and George. John Hyrne became the sole owner of the property after the deaths of Daniel and George.

John Hyrne Tucker was born on July 19, 1780. As a young man he suffered smallpox and was left with a face scarred from the pits of the sores. His blue-veined nose was of enormous size. But Tucker's appearance in no way impaired his opportunities for success in business and marriage. He acquired a great fortune, and during his life he married four times. On his death in June 1859, he left Litchfield Plantation to a son, Dr. Henry Massingberd Tucker. Henry had been born in 1831 to John's third wife. Henry studied medicine and graduated from the South Carolina College at Columbia in 1851. Some member of almost every planter's family practiced medicine. Planters' sons were urged to study "physic," as "you can then save yourself the expense of doctors' bills on your plantation, and in your family," according to the mistress of a local plantation. And, like Dr. Tucker, most of the young physicians had done their medical study at the South Carolina College at Columbia.

Dr. Henry Tucker married Annie Manigault. The couple had several children. The Tuckers owned a home "on the bay" in Charleston, and they spent time there during the winters when the crops were in. They also went there during hot summer months when it was considered unsafe to remain close to the rice fields, which bred mosquitoes. (Although it was not safe for the white people to remain on the plantations during the hot days, the slaves were considered immune to the malaria fever derived from the bites of mosquitoes.) In Charleston, the Tuckers attended the St. Cecilia balls and the Jockey Club ball, the latter winding up the horse-racing season.

Dr. Tucker was an Episcopalian and believed that the most proper place from which to go to heaven was the Episcopal Church. Litchfield Plantation was located adjacent to the property of All Saints Episcopal Church, and when the parishioners built a new church at All Saints, Dr. Tucker had the old church building dismantled and moved to his plantation down the road. Plantation services for slaves were held in that building, and any slave who failed to answer the roll call at services did not receive his weekly allotment of pork, sugar, molasses, and tobacco unless illness had prevented his attendance.

Along with other local planters, Dr. Tucker joined clubs established for purposes of companionship. One such club was the Pee Dee Club and another was the Hot and Hot Fish Club, an unlikely name since the club was organized as a means to give the planters a place to gather and discuss their crops and the latest news of politics.

Dr. Tucker enjoyed pure, physical exercise in the open air. He believed such exercise was essential to "the health." He also took delight in riding a horse over his vast properties. But the sport of hunting wild animals and other game seemed to give him more pleasure than almost anything else. Thanks to his keen eyes, he could shoot accurately, and he trained dogs to search out the game birds he killed. He owned so many guns that he gave them names, and he won so many tournaments at the Georgetown Rifle Club that he finally declined invitations to participate in the competition.

Along with all his sporting activities, social life, and the practice of medicine, Dr. Tucker bestowed upon his family abundant attention and consideration. No better illustration of this can be given than the way in which he entered his home after a late-night medical call. Dr. Tucker was often summoned from his bed to make a call to a sickbed in the community. When he arrived home in the middle of the night, he would tap the gatehouse bell with his riding crop, and after the gateman had opened the gate, Dr. Tucker would get off his horse and walk to the mansion. In order not to disturb his family, he would go to his room on the second floor by way of a small, circular stairway he had constructed in a portion of the mansion that was away from the other bedrooms.

When the Civil War came, Dr. Tucker, like other Low Country planters, volunteered his services. He served as an officer and a gallant soldier throughout the four years of that war. He surrendered with Lee at Appomattox.

After the war, Dr. Tucker faced the problems of Reconstruction, but during this time he attended to the medical needs of the community as before. When he arrived home in the middle of the night, he tapped the gatehouse bell with his riding crop, then made his way to the mansion, going to his room on the second floor by way of the circular stairway.

Dr. Henry Massingberd Tucker died on January 10, 1904, and was laid to rest in the cemetery at Prince George Winyah Episcopal Church in Georgetown. At about the time of the death of Dr. Tucker, the days of fortunes based on rice culture were coming to an end.

One night shortly after Dr. Tucker's death, something mysterious happened. During the night, when the rain had been of long duration and moisture had gathered on the oaks and seeped down into the Spanish moss and dripped to the lane under the trees, the bell at the gate suddenly rang as though it had been tapped by a riding crop. The sound of the bell echoed in the avenue under the giant trees near the mansion. The people who lived nearby, half asleep, thought that Dr. Tucker had returned to Litchfield from a call to a sickbed.

That eerie incident was repeated each night thereafter. Some said that the ghost of Dr. Tucker had returned to Litchfield. Others claimed that the wind, the moisture, or the chill of the night was responsible for the ringing. Whatever the cause, there were many who waited in dread for that one chime each night. When the bell rang, for a moment all their fears rushed forward. But then, since they knew the ringing was over for the night, their heartbeats slowed and their mouths were not so dry. They could settle down, knowing they wouldn't hear from the invisible caller for another twenty-four hours.

But the gatehouse bell rings no more. Litchfield Plantation is now a private residential development complete with villas, condominiums, private homes, a pool, a stable, and a marina on a Waccamaw River inlet. The manor house sits magnificently as it did in Dr. Tucker's day. Black wrought-iron gates by a brick gatehouse guard the entranceway. But the people around Litchfield Plantation can rest each night undisturbed, no longer tormented by that one, spine-tingling chime. The bell has been dismantled and taken away.

Alice, the Ghost of The Hermitage

from *More Tales of the South Carolina Low Country*
by Nancy Rhyne

Dr. Allard Flagg moved into his new home, The Hermitage, on Murrells Inlet, in 1849 and invited his widowed mother and his sister Alice to live with him. With delicate features, luminous brown eyes, and thick auburn hair that hung to her waist, Alice was a girl of unusual beauty.

Alice had not shown any interest in a beau, but her older brother Allard was beginning to cast interested glances toward Penelope Bentley Ward, and her other brother, Dr. Arthur Flagg, was openly courting Penelope's sister, Georgianna Ward.

The Wards of Brookgreen Plantation were the most noted of the planter families in the Low Country during the late 1840s. The amount of rice and oats cultivated by the Wards on their various plantations amounted to millions of pounds, and the vegetables grown in the gardens were harvested in enormous amounts. Each year several thousand bushels of corn, peas, beans, and sweet potatoes were brought from the large gardens. The

Wards also had a salt-making system on the nearby seashore, which was capable of producing from thirty to forty bushels of salt per day.

The rector of All Saints Episcopal Church at Pawleys Island considered the Wards among his most devoted and loyal parishioners, and all other planter families in the parish looked up to the Wards as far as achievement and prestige were concerned. So when word spread that Dr. Allard Flagg was interested in Penelope and Dr. Arthur Flagg considered Georgianna his best friend, no one thought a thing of it. It was a natural course of events.

Alice Flagg was pleased that her brothers had chosen cultured young women of good taste as their friends, and she delighted in the merrymaking that prevailed when the Ward girls came to The Hermitage. But as for Alice, prestige, achievement, culture, and good taste weren't the only qualities to look for when considering someone to marry. And for this, she had someone in mind.

One day a handsome young man came to call on Miss Alice. She had met him when she was shopping one day. Tall Dr. Allard met the man in the flower garden under a huge spreading oak tree and at once came to the conclusion from his speech, manners, profession, and background that the man was not suitable to be a friend of his sister. The caller was sent away without even a word with Miss Alice.

Alice was outraged, and Dr. Allard tried to console her. "Alice," he said, "he is not a professional man. He is a common turpentine dealer. Can't you see that if you choose him as a friend you will be choosing beneath yourself?"

"No!" Alice screamed defiantly. "He has an honorable profession. Don't you recognize the potential of a profession in the pine trees of this region?"

"Yes," Dr. Allard answered. "But in spite of that, the young man is beneath the notice of a Flagg. Let me hear no more about it!"

But Alice was not to be cowed, and she secretly kept in touch with her friend. After several weeks had passed, she boldly invited him to visit her again at The Hermitage. He agreed to come and told Alice that he would take her for a ride in his buggy, pulled by a team of fine bay horses.

He arrived early in the afternoon and was ushered by a servant into the imposing drawing room of The Hermitage. In a few minutes, Alice descended the staircase in the hallway and hurried into the drawing room. She did not disguise her happiness over seeing her friend. They left the drawing room and went to the wide porch and down the steps, where Alice's beau helped her into his carriage. Just as the suitor was ready to step up into the other side, Dr. Allard appeared on the porch. "Wait!" he cried out.

He ran down the steps, pushed the young man aside, and got into the buggy beside his sister, taking the reins. "I have sent someone to bring my horse," Dr. Allard said. "You'll ride the horse. I'll ride in the carriage with Alice. You may ride beside us and talk to Alice." The young man reluctantly agreed to the arrangement, but there was very little conversation between him and Alice that afternoon as they rode along, he on the horse, she in the carriage with her brother.

Dr. Allard, Dr. Arthur, and their mother had a family meeting, and it was decided that Alice would not be permitted to see her friend again. In the meantime her friend had secretly met her and slipped a ring on her finger and told her to consider it an engagement ring. She was ecstatic. They were very much in love.

When Dr. Allard saw the ring, he demanded that Alice remove it and give it to him so he could return it to the young man. She removed the ring, promising that she would return it, but she slipped it on a ribbon and tied the ribbon around her neck, concealing the ring beneath the collar of her dress.

In another family meeting, it was decided that Alice would be sent to Charleston to attend school so that she would forget about her beau. This was against her wishes, and she went reluctantly, but there was nothing she could do about it.

Alice cried for hours before she unpacked her trunk. She disliked everything she'd ever heard of Charleston: the mansions set far back from the bay, the almost-noble aristocracy, the societies that afforded merriment for the upper class, and most of all, the school where she was now stuck! Tears ran down her cheeks and fell on her dress, the one she treasured above all others, the soft white one with a wide ruffle that served as a collar as well as sleeves, for it draped over her shoulders and arms to her elbows. When she had finished unpacking, she pushed her trunk under the bed. It was only then that she looked around the room that she was to occupy. The bed looked comfortable, but the curtains were of a coarse gauze, and the entire room lacked color. It lacked *warmth*. Everything was so different in Charleston, and she missed her young man so much.

Several weeks passed before Alice began to get accustomed to the city. The pace wasn't quite so leisurely as at Murrells Inlet, and the sounds were startling. There was much screaming and talking when the fishing fleets came in at sunset, some of the fishermen taking care of the sails and cleaning the boats while others prepared the fish for market. Other sounds that surprised Alice were the street cries. Shrimp men chanted, "Shrimpy-raw-raw," while vegetable women carried their products in huge baskets balanced on their heads as they called out, "Vejjy-tuble, vejjy-tuble!" Then there was the rattle of empty milk tins being taken from doorways and full ones left in their places, the ice wagon and the *clop, clop* of the robust horses that pulled it, and the fire engine's clanging bell as it rushed to a fire. She could hear the chimney sweeps on the roofs and the lamplighters in the evenings. Though Alice did her best to adjust to Charleston and apply herself at school, she did not forget her turpentine dealer back home for one minute. Although he was considered to be "beneath the notice of a Flagg," she loved him with all her heart. Many times a day she pressed a hand to her chest to make sure her ring was still hanging on the ribbon around her neck.

Late one night, after attending a ball at the St. Cecilia Society, Alice became ill. The physician concluded that she was afflicted with malarial fever. Her family must be notified immediately, he told the school authorities.

When word of Alice's illness reached Dr. Allard Flagg, he left The Hermitage at once for Charleston in his carriage. By the time he reached Alice's bedside, she was delirious. Dr. Allard gave her some medication and ordered that her trunk be packed. He was taking her home to The Hermitage.

The journey to Murrells Inlet was not an easy one. It was raining, and the sky was dark with heavy clouds. There were seven rivers to be crossed by ferry, and the roadways were sand and the edges ill-defined, causing the carriage to slip into a ditch at times. Finally, Dr. Allard arrived at the avenue of oaks leading to The Hermitage. When the frail girl was lifted from the carriage, her brother saw that she was much, much worse.

Alice Flagg drifted into and out of consciousness all night long. Sometime during that first night she was back in her home in Murrells Inlet, she reached for the ring on the ribbon. It was not there! She begged, weakly, "I want my ring. Give me my ring." But her ring was not returned to her. By morning she was dead.

The body of Alice Flagg was dressed in her favorite white dress, and she was buried in the Flagg family plot at All Saints Cemetery near Pawleys Island. A plain marble slab was placed over her grave. Only one word is on the slab—*ALICE*.

Many times since the death of Alice Flagg there have been accounts of her being seen at The Hermitage. She comes in the front door and moves silently up the staircase to the bedroom that belonged to her. Sometimes she comes early in the evening, and at other times she makes her visits late at night. Also, it is said, she has been seen in the ancient graveyard at All Saints Church. But wherever she is seen, she always seems to be searching for something, while holding her hand over her chest.

The Holy Ghost Shell

from *Outer Banks Tales to Remember*
by Charles Harry Whedbee

For literally hundreds of years, beachcombing and shell collecting have been pleasant hobbies for both visitors and permanent residents of North Carolina's Outer Banks. Children and adults alike enjoy searching for the beautiful shells found in abundance on the seashore. Some people have amassed large collections. There are even shops that specialize in nothing but shells, both local and foreign.

One of the most popular of these shells is known as the sand dollar. Circular in shape and of various sizes, this skeleton of a small marine animal bleaches out to a pleasing whiteness on the beach and makes an interesting decoration or conversation piece. In the old days they were quite easy to find, but with the advent of millions of tourists and surf fishermen, they are becoming harder and harder to come by. It is now a fairly rare occurrence to find a perfect and unbroken sand dollar on the beach.

Most beach visitors know the sand dollar, but many of them have never heard the legend of that particular seashell, a legend that dates back to the early beginnings of English efforts to colonize this "goodliest soile under the cope of heaven."

When Amadas and Barlowe were sent to explore the land in April of 1584, they brought with them a sizable force of Englishmen to conduct the exploration. It is said that one of the sailors was a man named Henry Fowlkes who was, by nature, of a religious bent. He had even studied to be a priest in the newly formed Anglican Church.

Fowlkes was much impressed with the beauty of the land he was visiting, and he loved to take long, solitary walks along the golden beaches to meditate and to commune with his God. The local Indians were quite friendly and he had no fear of them, but he did not know that the Outer Banks, even then, were visited by upland tribes for the wonderful hunting and fishing they knew they would find. Some of these visitors came from the Iroquoian tribes far to the west, and they were much more warlike and fierce than the local Algonquins. As luck would have it, Fowlkes happened one day on one of these hunting parties and was promptly taken prisoner.

When the hunting party returned to their own village, they took the Englishman with them, and there he remained as a slave, as spring and summer faded into fall and winter. In time he learned the Iroquoian language and taught some of them to speak English, but he was looked down upon as a "squaw man," who was relegated to the most menial tasks and who could expect nothing but contempt.

After he taught them his language, the Englishman began to teach the tribe about Jesus and about his coming to save all mankind, including the Indians. He told them of the crucifixion and the resurrection of the Savior. As his lessons progressed, his audience became larger and larger. Some of the women began to inquire how they too could secure this salvation and life eternal. Even the fierce braves began to be interested and to ask searching questions.

The medicine men were infuriated. They saw a threat in this Englishman and his new religion. They greatly feared that their influence would fade away if the Indians accepted Christianity. These ritualists were men of considerable power in the tribe. Using the threat of vengeance by the forest spirits if these teachings were allowed to continue, they persuaded the chiefs to sentence Fowlkes to death for heresy. They insisted that he be taken back to the spot where he had been captured and there be beaten to death with their ceremonial clubs.

Accordingly, in the month of April in the year 1585, a party of braves carried the slave back to the very spot on the beach where he had been found. He was made to kneel in the wet sand, and the medicine men gathered around with their clubs, waiting for the Indian king to strike the first blow.

"Now, white man," intoned the king, "your God and your Jesus-brave know where to find you. Your Holy Ghost must know that this is the spot from which we took you. Call on your gods, and if they are as powerful as you say, ask them for a sign. Give us a sign from nature as our Great Spirit does for us when we pray. Do this and we will release you. Pray, bearded-face! Pray for a sign or you die!"

Believing that death was imminent, Fowlkes clasped his hands and prayed with all his might that he be delivered from dying on this foreign shore, never to see his beloved England again. He was man enough and Christian enough to conclude his prayer with the very words of our Savior, "Father, if it be thy will, let this cup pass from me. Nevertheless, not my will but thine be done."

Snarling, a medicine man kicked the kneeling slave in the face and sent him sprawling into the sand. "He speaks of a cup," sneered the Indian. "Let him drink from the cup of death."

As he struggled to rise from the sand, Fowlkes' hand closed around a large sand dollar. He had not seen such a seashell before, as they are common only on the sandy beaches of North America. He gazed upon it with awe.

"See, see," he shouted, holding the shell up before the chief's face. "Here is your sign. See how this strange shell shows forth the very things I told you about my Lord. See the circular shape like the crown of thorns. See the five slashes—they represent the thorns that pierced His brow. See the five marks in the center of the shell, which show the five wounds my Savior received on the cross. Here is your sign. Only see. See and believe!"

Taking the shell in his trembling hands, the chief turned it over and over and examined it from every angle. As a frequenter of this coast he had seen many of these shells and had wondered about the markings but had never had anyone try to explain them to him. Here, indeed, was the "sign from nature" he demanded of the white man.

The head shaman was staring open-mouthed in amazement, not knowing what to say. The chief turned to hand him the shell, and in the exchange between the hands of the two, the fragile shell broke in half. Out fell several little things that looked exactly like little white doves.

"There is the sign of the Holy Ghost," exulted the prisoner. "This is not the Holy Ghost itself but is a sign—a sign using the image of that same white dove that descended bringing the Comforter to the people until my Lord's coming again."

The legend concludes that the tribesmen then turned and fled the beach and returned with all haste to their village, leaving the Englishman alone upon the strand. It is also said that this may be one explanation of the smattering of Christianity that the early settlers found extant among the inland Indians.

Fowlkes lost no time in walking down the beach to a point opposite Roanoke Island, where he found, to his joy, that Sir Richard Grenville had just arrived with some 600 men and would soon return to England. Sir Richard welcomed Henry Fowlkes as an additional hand on board one of his ships and carried him back to his native land, where Fowlkes entered the Anglican priesthood and spent the rest of his life serving churches in Devon and Yorkshire. He is said to have carried many sand dollars with him and to have used them in his sermons.

Now, you may know that the sand dollars found on the Atlantic and Pacific shores of this country are really specimens of the various thin, circular echinoderms of the order *Clypeastrina*, especially *Echinarachnius parma*, of sandy ocean bottoms of the northern Atlantic and Pacific. But ask any knowledgeable coastal child what one is, and like a little cherub, he will explain to you that it is really the Holy Ghost shell and that his grandfather has shown him the marks of the thorns and wounds. If it is a whole shell, he might break it in two for you and let you see the little snow-white doves that come from the inside.

Imagery? Superstition? Well, now, don't be too sure. "There are more things in this world than are dreamed of in your philosophy."

The Wicked Witch of Nantahala

from *Mountain Ghost Stories and Curious Tales of Western North Carolina*
by Randy Russell and Janet Barnett

In days long past, there were more than snarling bears and mountain panthers to frighten children in the hills of western North Carolina. There was Spearfinger, a woman-monster who fed on human livers.

Spearfinger, a singularly nasty witch known to the Cherokee, feasted on unsuspecting children throughout the mountains. She was, however, particularly associated with Whiteside Mountain, a prominent peak at an elevation of 4,950 feet, one side of which is a highly visible 1,800-foot sheer cliff. This solid rock face is the highest exposed-rock cliff in the eastern United States.

In this part of the Nantahala National Forest just off U.S. Highway 64 between Cashiers and Highlands, the mountain woods are thick with towering hemlocks and spruce.

Banks of the stream near Whiteside are quilted with moss and criss-crossed with the delicate lace of thriving ferns. But it's the rocks that contribute most to the visual drama of Whiteside Mountain.

The area is littered with rocks. A jutting formation on the east side of Whiteside Mountain is known locally as the Devil's Courthouse, while a particularly large boulder about halfway up the same outcropping of rocks is claimed to be Satan's throne.

It was from these very rocks that the witch Spearfinger sprang. A terrifying witch, Spearfinger possessed the power to take on any appearance she chose, including that of the rocks. In her true form, Spearfinger looked something like an old woman, with some notable differences.

The ancient witch, who outlived generation upon generation of man, was yellowish in appearance. Her entire body was covered by a hard skin of rock, a skin so dense it proved impenetrable by arrow or ax. Spearfinger could best be identified by the form of her right hand, one finger of which was long and pointed, resembling an awl. The witch used her finger to fatally stab anyone unlucky enough to come within the range of her sharpened reach.

In her true form, the vicious witch also possessed a strong, horrible smell, which she could at times mask when people came near. Yet her natural malodorous state was so severe that Spearfinger was crawling with flies. Among the Cherokee, it was known that the hum of flies in the mountain forest meant that Spearfinger might be hiding somewhere nearby.

When hungry, Spearfinger altered her appearance to that of a sweet old lady, the flies vanishing, her stone skin disguised. The evil witch had enormous powers over stone and could easily move huge rocks. She could cement two stones together simply by striking one against the other. And she could turn herself into stone to keep from being found in the rocky terrain of the mountains.

To travel through the rugged country more easily, Spearfinger set about building a great bridge between Whiteside Mountain and a distant peak. The bridge was well under way when it was struck by lightning. The fragments of Spearfinger's stone bridge were scattered at the base of Whiteside Mountain. Pieces of her bridge are still visible today throughout the region.

Spearfinger favored hiding at the heads of mountain streams and in the dark passes and hollows of the Nantahala Gorge, where other Indian evils were known to lurk. She ventured throughout the area in search of her favorite food, however, and anyone who came across her in the mountains was a likely victim of her ferocious appetite for human livers. Spearfinger was especially fond of children.

At the time of Spearfinger, the rich bottomlands of the Nantahala National Forest were noted for their abundance of strawberries and other wild fruits and berries. Cherokee children were often sent into the hollows and grassy areas along the rushing streams to pick wild strawberries for their village. The children were especially vulnerable at these times. Many were snatched away by Spearfinger.

At other times, when no child could be found at the wooded edges of the rocky mountain forests, Spearfinger would venture closer to the villages, watching with hungry eyes from behind a tattered shawl for any child she might be able to seize.

Spearfinger would call to the children, referring to them as her grandchildren. There is no word for grandchild in the Cherokee language. Cherokee endearingly addressed their grandchildren as "my son's children" or "children of my daughter." The endearment was particularly alluring when spoken by a kind old lady with gray hair who hid her smile behind a shawl.

"Come," Spearfinger would call. "Come, my little girl, and let your grandmother dress your hair."

The witch hid her mouth because her teeth were made of sharp, broken pieces of stone that would scare the children away.

She was also careful to keep her awl finger hidden beneath her shawl. When one of the girls ambled over, the wicked witch laid the child's head in her lap. She petted and combed the child's hair with the fingers of her other hand until the little darling fell fast asleep.

Then, with her rock-and-bone finger, the hungry witch stabbed the napping child through the heart. Spearfinger quickly removed the child's liver with her blood-smeared awl finger and ate it on the spot. As the old witch chewed, she gradually returned to her true form, her skin hardening and taking on its yellow cast, the fetid smell rising as flies came to light upon her wretched, laughing face.

Warriors would follow the trail of buzzing flies and drying blood into the dense forest, but with no result. Spearfinger simply changed herself into a pile of rocks or a single boulder whenever anyone came after her. After the murder of village children, she was occasionally discovered in the form of stone by Cherokee warriors when a particular boulder or human-sized pile of stones was covered with flies. But the warriors could do little to harm the witch. Many arrows and spears were broken in an attempt to kill Spearfinger after she'd changed herself into a rock. Should the warrior touch the rock, he'd be tainted with the smell of the witch as if he'd been sprayed by a skunk, and he would have to sleep outside his home for at least four days before he was permitted to enter again. The unlucky Cherokee spent those four days fighting off flies.

Cherokee children were particularly vulnerable to attack in autumn. This was the time of leaf burning, when the Cherokee burned fallen leaves from the forest floor before shaking chestnuts from the tees. The old witch was always on the lookout for trails of smoke among the trees of the Nantahala Forest in autumn. She knew that the children of the villages would be gathering the nuts and wandering to the edges of the mountainside. The wrinkled crone would patiently wait, sharpening her appetite, waiting to change into a gentle old grandmother and surprise a hapless child who was accidentally separated from the others. Cherokee elders, the actual grandparents of the children, tried diligently to keep the children together as they gathered chestnuts.

The witch of Whiteside Mountain became a pronounced danger when she could find no children in the forests on whom to dine. She ventured progressively closer to the villages, watching with hungry eyes from behind her tattered shawl for any child she might be able to seize. Spearfinger might ultimately summon her powers and enter a village in search of a meal. She'd wait until she spied a family member leaving a house. Instantly, the hungry witch took on the appearance of the family member and entered the home. So swift was Spearfinger and so sharp her finger that at these times she could stab a child without the victim's even knowing it. The witch left no wound and caused no pain, quickly removing the liver and carrying it off into the night, where she could eat it in safety while slowly changing back to her yellowed form. The child who was her victim went about his affairs until all at once he felt weak and grew ill. Eventually, the child pined away and died because Spearfinger had stolen from his small body its tender liver.

On rare occasions a solitary hunter spotted Spearfinger walking in the forest. Her hand was visible even from a distance, appearing at first glance as if she were carrying a knife. No hunter came too near because the strong odor of Spearfinger warned him off.

The witch was said to sing along with the hum of the flies that accompanied her as she walked among the rocks and trees, climbing carefully up the mountainside. It was rather a pretty song, sung in a low voice like a lullaby, but one that told of the many sweet livers of children

Spearfinger had consumed. More than one hunter lifted his bow and arrow, his blood chilled by the words of the witch's song, and took aim at the dreadful creature, only to watch his arrow bounce off her hardened skin or break in two upon contact. The hunter would then hurry away in silent fright back to his village to tell his story of Spearfinger.

So many children died in the area of Whiteside Mountain that the Cherokee called a great council to devise a manner to rid the forest of the wicked she-monster before everyone was killed. Indians traveled from many villages to attend the council. After much debate, it was decided that the best way to kill Spearfinger was to trap her in a pitfall. Then all the warriors could attack her at once.

The pitfall was known among nearly all the Indians of the eastern United States, but was used only to catch especially large or dangerous game. A pit was dug along a trail and covered with underbrush. The animal was chased along the trail until it stumbled upon the pitfall and fell snarling into the deep trap.

The Cherokee dug a pit across the trail outside their village and covered it with leaves, twigs, and small, brittle branches. They were careful to line the trail with similar autumn leaves so that Spearfinger would not discern that the ground had been disturbed. To entice the witch, the Indians lit a fire on the other side of the trail before hiding themselves in the shrubbery.

Spearfinger saw the trail of smoke and smacked her lips. She believed the children had been sent out from the village to gather chestnuts. The witch made her way down Whiteside Mountain.

The hidden warriors waited. Eventually, an old woman wearing a shawl came along the trail. Several of the young men wanted to shoot her upon sight, but the closer she came the more it appeared that this old woman with gray hair might not be the wicked witch they meant to kill. In fact, she looked exactly like an old woman of the village they all knew well.

After some hushed debate, the warriors let the woman pass unmolested. If she were the woman from the village, she would know they'd built a pitfall, they reasoned. The Indians had already pointed out to each other that this elderly woman kept her right hand covered by her shawl.

With a loud crash, Spearfinger tumbled into the pitfall. Upon landing at the bottom of the deep hole, she changed instantly into her true, yellow form. A swarm of late-season flies followed her into the pit. No longer a feeble old woman, the stony-skinned Spearfinger snarled and raged in a rasping, terrible voice as the warriors encircled the pit, weapons poised. She ranted curses upon the Cherokee around the sharp, broken rocks that were her teeth. The odor of the witch was so strong that many of the warriors had to back away from the rim of the pit after firing an arrow at the yellow witch.

The battle had just begun. The savage liver-eater scrambled up one side of the pit, then the other, reaching out with her bone finger in all directions, looking for someone to stab. The warriors beat Spearfinger back by throwing large rocks, but they did no damage other than to cause the woman-monster to fall back down into the hole.

The warriors grew frantic. Though they fired their arrows straight and true and as rapidly as they were able, the weapons proved useless against Spearfinger's stony skin. The arrows broke and fell like snapped twigs all around the witch.

Spearfinger taunted the men, certain she would eventually climb out of the pit and get at them. A small bird the Cherokee call *tsi-kilili*, the Carolina chickadee, watched from a nearby spruce branch and began to sing to the warriors. The Cherokee know the chickadee as a truth teller. The bird swooped into the pit, singing, "Here, here, here." The chickadee bravely alighted on the yellow witch's deadly finger, and try as she might Spearfinger could not shake it loose. The warriors understood that *tsi-kilili* was instructing them to fire the arrows at her right hand. They did so, and as an arrow struck the witch's palm she let out a piercing scream. Her wounded hand poured forth a great quantity of blood.

The chickadee lifted in flight as the old witch withered and died.

Many demons and witches of the mountains were known to hide their hearts in secret places so they couldn't be killed. Spearfinger always kept her right hand clenched because she carried her heart in her hand. *Tsi-kilili* had somehow learned Spearfinger's secret, and the small bird remains a welcome friend among the Cherokee.

The witch was buried where she lay, at the bottom of the pit. Some believe Spearfinger turned herself into one of the rocks in the pitfall and lived to stalk today.

It is still considered a foreboding of bad luck when a fly is found buzzing around a rock in the Nantahala National Forest in autumn. Cherokee hunters will change direction to keep from hiking beyond such a spot. The warning is considered especially severe if the fly is seen in November, long after the killing October frosts have turned the leaves.

Blackbeard's Cup

from *Blackbeard's Cup and Stories of the Outer Banks*
by Charles Harry Whedbee

"They say" that you should never tell a story in the first person. "They say" that it robs the story of some of its interest and that the teller limits himself unnecessarily. Well, "they" apparently have never heard of the popularity of true confession magazines and the appeal of the "I was there" approach. Anyway, there are some stories that cannot well be told in any other way.

The time was the very early nineteen-thirties, right in the middle of the late and unlamented "Great Depression." Nags Head and the remainder of the Outer Banks were still the "best kept secret" in North Carolina. There were miles and miles of undeveloped beaches on both the sound and the ocean sides of the famous barrier reef, and the whole area was as close to being a modern-day Garden of Eden as it could be. I was, at the time, a student in the law school at the University of North Carolina and already a veteran of nearly twenty summers of roaming and loving the Outer Banks.

Also in the same law school at the time was a young man who shall be known here only as Jack to preserve his anonymity. He, also, was an habitué of this golden strand since childhood and was a member of one of the finest families in eastern North Carolina. At that time Jack was even more conversant with the legends of the region than I, particularly the regions around Ocracoke and Portsmouth Island. A lifelong friendship had grown between us, and we young blades spent countless happy and carefree days exploring these sands and drinking to the full the mystery and wonder of the area.

This was the picture on that happy August day when Jack came to me and said, "Charlie, I hope you've got ten dollars to spare because that will be your share of the cost of hiring a gas boat to take us to Ocracoke to-morrow as well as board and lodging for one night." I hadn't known we were going to Ocracoke at all, much less on the morrow but at that age in life, "theirs was not to reason why." After all, what was there to lose be-sides a lazy summer day? It put a tremendous dent in my pocketbook but I just happened to have that amount on hand so, without question, the deal was made and the trip planned. I had no idea what Jack had in mind, but a trip to Ocracoke was pleasant at any time and even then the price seemed a bargain.

Why not a car? In those days very few people could afford a car, and most of the ones who were affluent enough to try the trip over land and inlet usually got stuck in the sand. The ferries were adequate for the traf-fic at the time, but such an undertaking was fraught with danger and delay and frequent calls to the Coast Guard for an overland rescue. No, a boat was slower sometimes, but usually very pleasant and more dependable. Given the wind direction and force and the type and location of the clouds, you could estimate the time of your arrival at any given point on Albemarle or Pamlico Sounds with fairly reasonable accuracy.

The next day dawned clear and mild, and an early departure from the long pier jutting out from Hollowell's Store and Post Office into the sound was made with high spirits and keen anticipation. There was no shade or awning on the Dutch Net boat we had hired and no relief from the blaz-ing August sun, but all the voyagers were young and strong and already tanned a deep mahogany, so it made little difference. After all, who knew what adventure might lie ahead? We had practically no money to spare, but we were young and almost disgustingly healthy and it was summer and we were at Nags Head! The copious lunch we took along was consumed before the sun reached the zenith and the trip southward was without notable event. After we ate, we rescued some chicken bones from the drumsticks, threaded them onto hooks, attached a crab line we found in the boat, and trolled for bluefish. We caught a fairly nice mess of fish which we gave to our "skipper."

Ocracoke landfall was made well before dark, and the smooth water of Silver Lake beckoned us to a safe landing at the pier. The short walk to the Pamlico Inn was rewarded by the usual cordial welcome from the Gaskills and we settled in for supper.

After a bountiful seafood supper, we stepped out into the gathering dusk of a beautiful Ocracoke evening and breathed deeply of the soft, salty breeze which was coming in from the eastwards. Up to that point I had not known that there was any special purpose to our journey. Just a trip "down to Ocracoke" with all its nostalgic sights and sounds and smells was reason enough, not to mention the wonderful people who were part and parcel of it all. Pleasures were simple at that time and in that place but they were deep and soul satisfying. Even in those days it was like stepping back into history. That was part of the magic of Ocracoke.

"Come on," said Jack, "we don't want to be late." When I demanded to know where we were going, he said, "To the castle." "Are you crazy?" I asked. "Shell castle is out yonder in the middle of the sound and Jasper, our skipper, won't be back until tomorrow morning!" "Take it easy, Chuck," he replied. "There's more than one castle around here, and the one we're going to is Blackbeard's castle. Come on with me."

On we went down the picture-book streets of the town in the direction of Silver Lake. There were places where the branches of the trees met overhead, forming a sort of fragrant tunnel through which we walked. Jack apparently knew the way, and it seemed to me we walked a good while before we came to a large, white clapboard house with a sort of cupola or lookout tower on top, overlooking the waters of the sound. "This is it!" whispered Jack. "Look alive now and do exactly as I do and we may see something very few people ever get to see."

Walking across the broad front porch, Jack knocked three times on the huge door with his clenched fist. The door swung slowly open, just enough for me to see a large, lantern-lit room and the silhouette of a tremendous, bearded man peering cautiously out of the cracked door.

"What is it you want?" growled the giant. To my amazement, Jack immediately answered, "Death to Spotswood." The eyes of the bear flashed to me. "And you?" he asked. Flabbergasted, I stammered the same thing Jack had said or as close to it as I could manage. That apparently, was some sort of password, because the heavy door swung open and we walked in. Only my unwillingness to leave Jack in such a spot prevented me from bolting for the door and back to the inn as fast as I could run.

The room we entered had obviously been used at one time as a dining room or banquet room. With high ceilings and beautiful wood paneling, its only furnishings now consisted of a very large oak table in the middle of the room surrounded by a number of rather modern-looking bentwood chairs. The only illumination came from a huge kerosene lantern placed in the middle of the table. Its soft, warm light revealed about a dozen of the biggest, toughest-looking men I had ever seen. Most of them were heavily bearded with flashing blue eyes, and every one of them spoke with that Elizabethan inflection so usual on this coast, which has been called "hoi toide talk."

As the first order of business, Jack and I were required to place our hands on a large Bible and to take a solemn oath that, under penalty of death, we would not reveal anything that went on in that room that night for thirty-five years. With a shiver of mixed anticipation and apprehension, I took the oath and settled back into one of the chairs near the table. Jack did likewise. The others in the room did not take the oath but they took similar seats and for a short while we heard nothing but the buzz of several different conversations.

All at once and as though on signal, an abrupt silence engulfed the room as a door at the far end swung slowly open and the bearded giant who had admitted us strode in, holding aloft a large, silver cup of a most peculiar shape. Handing it to the man at the head of the table, he sat down and the man holding the cup raised it ceilingward and in a deep resonant voice chanted, "Death to Spotswood!"——the same phrase that had gained us admission to the house. So saying, he took a long draught of the liquid in the cup and passed it to the man next to him, who did the same thing and said the same words. The cup then was passed from hand to hand around the table until it came to me. Thrusting the cup against my chest, my neighbor fixed me with a stare so fierce and so demanding that my knees began to quiver. Too afraid to do anything else, I lifted the cup as I had seen them do and, in the lowest voice I could muster, repeated the words. Lowering the cup, I drank a large swallow of the amber liquid. My mouth and throat burned as if on fire! I gagged and coughed and finally managed to swallow, while the eyes of all that group were upon me. The stuff had not seemed to bother them at all.

While the silver cup was in my hands and before I passed it to Jack, I noticed it was of a very peculiar shape. Much larger than any drinking cup or chalice I had ever seen, it was nearly so large as a punch bowl and was relatively shallow for its width. At two places on its lip there were cup-shaped depressions in the edge about three inches apart, which sloped inward and made drinking from that side of the cup very difficult. I had quickly discovered that the potion we were drinking was some of the strongest corn whiskey I had ever sampled. It had a kick like a Missouri mule and that first swallow almost floored me.

Well, the evening wore on and the cup made round after round of the huge table. Frankly, I was scared not to take my part in the goings on, but I took as small sips of the potent liquor as I thought I could get by with. After a few rounds of the table, the talk loosened up and became more informal, and that night I heard some of the wildest tales about Edward Teach, the pirate, you can imagine. By that time we were on a first-name basis, but I never once heard the surnames of any of those present.

Fairly early in the evening I was enlightened to the fact that the oblate spheroid shape of the cup was due to the cup's being the silver-plated skull of Blackbeard himself. I became a little queasy when it dawned on me that, if the cup was a skull, then the little dips in its lip had to be the eye sockets! Carved in rather rough Elizabethan letters around the outside of the cup were the words "DETH TO SPOTSWOODE." Just how long the wild tales and the loving cup lasted I have no idea. Jack and I made the excuse that we needed to go outside to get some fresh air. Once outside, we made the best speed we could to our lodgings and an exhausted sleep.

Jasper was back with his gas boat bright and early the next morning, and we made our way northward to Nags Head and a safe landing on the soundside. Little did we know that Blackbeard's castle and the Pamlico Inn and the Wahab house would be either destroyed or damaged beyond repair by the hurricane that struck Ocracoke in 1944, but such was to be the fate of these and several other well-known buildings on that historic island.

Afraid to discuss our adventure in front of Jasper, Jack and I waited until we were ashore before we started talking it out. We figured the oath did not forbid our discussing it with one another—only with nonpartici-pants. It turned out that Jack was almost as ignorant of what the strange affair meant and how it came to be as I was. A long-time "Banker" friend had given him the password and told him when and where to show up if he wanted to see something he probably would never see again. Acting on the trusted word of that friend, Jack had led us into the adventure.

We had both heard many times that Blackbeard's severed head had been coated with silver and made into a punch bowl and used by some Virginia families. We knew, of course, that the royal governor Spotswood, who had brought about Blackbeard's death, refused to return to England after his term of office expired because he feared (and probably rightly) that Blackbeard's friends, the Brethren of the Coast, would learn of it, intercept him at sea, and avenge the death of their friend and leader.

We kept our oath, Jack and I. At least, I feel sure that he did and I know that I did. It has now been more than fifty years and I figure I have done my part to keep their confidence. I can see no harm and no oath violation in disclosing this now. I don't even know whether any of the party who met that night is alive, but I do know the castle is no longer there.

In the trials and tribulations of pursuing a career in the law, the memory of the schoolboy adventure almost faded from my memory. One day re-cently I was looking through some old books I had inherited and I came across Crecy's *Grandfather's Tales of North Carolina History*, which was writ-ten back in the eighteen hundreds and was published by Edwards and Broughton. The author, Richard Benbury Crecy, lived closer to Blackbeard's time than we do, and he had devoted a section to the pirate. A perusal of the book proved Crecy to be a very accurate and a very complete por-trayer of the history of this state. In his chapter on Teach he writes:

Teach had seventeen desperate men under him. Maynard had more than thirty. The engagement was desperate. By a feint, Maynard's men were sent below and Teach was made to believe that Maynard declined the fight and was about to surrender. When Teach saw this, he sailed to Maynard's ship to take possession of her. As soon as he boarded, Maynard ordered his men on deck and then it was a hand to hand fight, Maynard and Teach heading it with sabers. Teach was mortally wounded after he had wounded twenty of Maynard's men. After Maynard had captured Teach's sloop, he cut off his head, fastened it to his bowsprit and sailed up to Bath in Beaufort County, then Hyde.

No mention here of carrying the head back to Virginia! And remember, Bath was Blackbeard's hometown. A great majority of the people there were his friends, including Governor Eden. In fact, Eden had performed Blackbeard's marriage ceremony just weeks before when he took a local bride. Maybe the severed head did not go to Virginia after all! Maybe it was "rescued" by some of the many friends of the pirate, and maybe it was them or some local silversmith who fashioned it into a silver cup bearing the curse on Spotswood. Perhaps the account of a punch bowl being made from the skull was a garbled one. What human has ever had a skull big enough to be used as a punch bowl? Maybe that odd-shaped, shallow bowl from which I drank was, indeed, the genuine article. Remember the secrecy with which it had been displayed and remember the location. Was it really the skull-bowl? I had to find out.

From that day to this I have tried as opportunity arose to trace the whereabouts and ownership of the bowl. Twice I thought I was on the verge of finding it, once in Norfolk and once in Virginia Beach, only to have the trail go cold. Both times it was rumored to be the property of a very rich Virginia collector, but when I tried as discreetly as I could to find him, I ran into a solid wall of silence.

I have discussed this search with my internist, a medical man in whom I have the utmost confidence, and he also has become interested. He tells me that if I can obtain possession of the object for only a few hours, he will help me have it X-rayed to determine if, indeed, there is a human skull underlying the silver plating. Before I meet my Maker I would greatly like to determine whether the silver bowl from which I drank is truly the skull of the famous pirate. The only way I know to do this is to obtain the cup so that it may be X-rayed, even if I am supervised and even if it is a brief loan.

In one final effort to do exactly that, I make this offer. I will pay one thousand dollars in cash to the person who loans me the cup from which I drank and I promise I will keep it just long enough to have it X-rayed. I will post a bond for its safe return and I pledge never to reveal the name and/or address of the owner. There is no chance of a counterfeit being run in on me. I held the cup in my hands and I drank from it and I shall immediately recognize it if I ever see it again. My friend Jack has long ago passed to his reward or I would certainly enlist his help in the search. Maybe, from where he is now, he already knows whether the cup is the genuine article, but I surely would like to know.

I surely would.

The Ghost Who Cried for Help

from *Haints, Witches, and Boogers: Tales from Upper East Tennessee*
by Charles Edwin Price

Boys the world over love to take dares—that's an undeniable fact. A night spent in a haunted house, or any other location supposedly infested by a ghost, is the kind of dare that no self-respecting young man can resist, especially when pressed by his peers. A favorite spot for this kind of sport in upper East Tennessee is a copse of a half-dozen elm and oak trees near Piney Flats, located about halfway between Johnson City and Bristol. There, the horrible apparition of a wounded Union soldier once pleaded piteously for help, his red eyes glowing with the fires of hell.

The legend of the ghost who cried for help had its beginnings in September 1863. Union troops under the command of General Ambrose Burnside set upon a force of Confederates assembled in Washington County. After a skirmish, Union troops retired, thinking they had soundly whipped the Confederates. A portion of the Union force was left to guard an important bridge across Little Limestone Creek, while the remaining soldiers returned to Greeneville by train.

The Confederates were not beaten quite so easily. Their ranks swelled by reinforcements from Jonesborough, they attacked the Yankees at the bridge. For a time, a Confederate victory seemed imminent. But Union troops increased their fire, aided by twelve-pound Napoleon smooth-bore cannons, and the Southerners were forced to retreat to the Greene County line.

Two weeks later, Confederate forces again engaged Union troops in and around Jonesborough, the county seat of Washington County. A running battle ensued that extended from Jonesborough northward through Johnson's Depot (later Johnson City) and on toward Bluff City. Scattered groups of men on both sides stalked each other, blazing away from behind trees, rock outcroppings, and riverbanks. Confederate sharpshooters, most of whom had gained their skills by hunting game in the woods back home, shot down Union soldiers like so many rabbits.

In a little grove of trees near Piney Flats, the story goes, three Union soldiers were ambushed by Confederates. When the smoke cleared, two soldiers lay dead and a third was gravely wounded. The sharpshooters moved on to other prey, leaving the wounded man to suffer all night, calling out piteously for someone to come help him. The sniper's minie ball had smashed through his right leg, severing an artery. The man ripped his shirt and applied a makeshift tourniquet, but the bleeding wouldn't stop. No one answered his calls for help, and by morning he was dead.

Several days later, the three bodies were discovered by neighborhood boys, who ran home to tell their parents of the grisly find. The dead soldiers were given a decent Christian burial, and the incident was soon forgotten.

A year later, a traveling sutler was passing the grove when he heard someone crying out for help. Not knowing about the ambush and the wounded soldier, he walked over to the trees to see if he could help. No one was there, but the sutler could still hear the voice, loud and clear in the twilight.

"Where are you?" the sutler asked.

The voice stopped. Nothing could be heard except the gentle rustling of the cold November wind.

The sutler decided that he must have been hearing things and continued on his way toward Piney Flats. When he arrived at the local tavern, he rounded up a friend to help him pop the cork from a fresh jug of liquor. A short time later, when both men were mellow, the sutler told his friend about the voice he had heard in the grove of trees. His companion suddenly grew silent.

"What's the matter?" the sutler asked.

"There was three Yankees killed up there about a year ago," his friend replied. "We found 'em a couple of days later, and we figure that one of 'em suffered some before he died, judgin' from the expression on his face. It might be his ghost that you heard."

It was the sutler's turn to fall silent. Then his friend, warm with fresh corn liquor, ventured a suggestion: "Why don't we ride up there and have a look?"

The sutler agreed, and his companion saddled two of his best horses. A half-hour later, jug still in hand, the two men stood next to the little grove of trees.

"I don't hear nothing," the friend said.

"Neither do I," replied the sutler, suddenly very nervous. "Let's go back. I suspect it's close to midnight, and I have to be on the road early in the morning."

As they turned to go, a voice behind them cried out, "Help me, help me! I'm bleedin' to death."

The sutler and his friend turned around. No one was in sight. "Help me, help me!" the voice called out again.

"It's coming from behind that boulder," the sutler said.

The two men crept to the rock and peered over. A soldier in a Union uniform lay on the ground holding his leg and trying to stop the bleeding. He looked real enough. And his predicament didn't seem far-fetched— after all, the war was still on. But just then, the soldier turned his head toward the sutler and his friend and grinned. His eyes were a glowing red.

The sutler headed at top speed in the opposite direction from Piney Flats, and without benefit of the horse he rode in on. He was never seen in that part of the country again.

His friend, who had more presence of mind, jumped on his horse and hurried back to town. When he returned to the tavern, he told everyone about the incident at the grove of trees. A group of curious townspeople visited the grove that very night, but no one saw or heard a thing. The consensus was that the sutler and his friend were merely suffering from a bad case of the "corn jitters."

But as in all stories of this sort, there exists a seed of plausibility. There *really was* a running Civil War skirmish through the area, and a few unlucky Yankee soldiers could easily have met their death in the little grove.

The copse is now part of a private farm, and the owner has posted No Trespassing signs around the property. But stern warnings do not deter those bent on derring-do. Today, when local boys get together to test their manhood, they goad each other into spending the night in the haunted copse near Piney Flats. Some gather enough courage to do so. Voices have been reported there over the years, but so far no one has seen the wounded soldier since that night so long ago when the sutler and his friend stared into the horrible red eyes of the ghost who cried for help.

Stede Bonnet

from *Blackbeard and Other Pirates of the Atlantic Coast*
by Nancy Roberts

In the late morning he rode his black stallion at a deliberate pace along the winding, dirt road of the plantation, fringed on either side with lush green banana plants. The tropical sky was an intense blue and the sun so bright it hurt Stede Bonnet's eyes—not surprisingly, because Stede Bonnet had a hangover. But it was not his fault. He was driven to drink by the boredom of this blasted place where one day was much like another. What excitement could there possibly be if a man never had to overcome danger or risk his life?

Barbados had all the appearance of a paradise, but to a man with a reckless, adventurous spirit, this island of cane and banana plantations, a civilization that had gone virtually unchanged for more than a century, was a provincial prison.

And if he should complain to his wife or his sisters, what would he say he wanted instead? What would they see as a reasonable alternative? Their reaction to his desire to leave the island would be one of horror and despair, but not so great as if he told them his *secret* desire.

Yet what was there to lose, he thought, for a man already dead within?

He turned his horse's head toward the Bridgetown dock as he was often wont to do. Captains of the ships taking on sugar, rum, molasses and more dubious cargo glanced at him curiously as he sat astride his black stallion watching them. A man in fitted black trousers and a loose white shirt with full sleeves, he was dressed a shade too flamboyantly. He had dark, curly hair, a suntanned skin and regular if not handsome features. The seagoing men who put in at Barbados knew *his* kind—a wealthy, pampered sugar plantation owner amusing himself; a scion of one of the English families who enjoyed a life of ease in the pleasant climate of this small South Atlantic island.

Barbados had only recently become a British colony. The war with Spain was over, and Governor Lowther represented the crown. The governor spent his time trying to encourage trade at Bridgetown harbor while discouraging the lawlessness that remained from the decade before; it had been here that dashing privateer captains, dressed in silk and velvet and ornamented with gold chains, had anchored to dispose of captured cargo.

Stede Bonnet, mounted on the black Arabian stallion, thought of those days on this sunny spring morning of 1717. Although to his fellow islanders Major Bonnet appeared to be a typical planter—the steady and responsible husband of Mary Allamby Bonnet and father of their children, Allamby, Edward, Stede, and Mary—in truth he was the very opposite. The staid example his father had set him in his youth had long ceased to do battle with a self of another sort, one who took wealth and ease as his right and now sought only excitement.

At twelve he had visualized himself as a swashbuckling knight-errant living by the sword. Many boys have such dreams but reject them with maturity; however, Stede was now twenty-eight and his admiration for men who seized what they wanted from life by force had not waned. It had become an obsession. In the afternoons he read, stared moodily at the masts of the ships in the distant harbor, or went down to the docks and sat astride his horse watching vessels come and go, daydreaming about adventure.

To anyone in such a state of mind, fate inevitably presents an opportunity to choose the course of his secret desire. So it was that Stede Bonnet learned of a vessel up for auction.

"Found deserted at sea without papers or crew," said the captain who brought her into port—an unlikely story! She had probably been taken in an act of piracy the year before. Major Stede Bonnet was high bidder. The major's wife and his friends in the port village were puzzled, but he explained that he had decided shipping would be a logical extension of his sugar and rum production.

Friends queried him hopefully. "Will you be buying rum or sugar from us? You will need more than you can supply from your own plantation, if you're to prosper in this venture."

He would smile mysteriously and make no reply. Major Stede Bonnet was planning to embark on a career of piracy. He knew what that meant. When a state of war does not exist, armed robbery at sea is regarded as a crime against all men. He would be an international outlaw—a criminal who could be tried and hanged anywhere in the world.

Although Bonnet knew nothing of seafaring, he hired a quartermaster who did, one Israel Morton, and Morton began to recruit men. Meanwhile, even Bonnet's wife did not realize that the sloop her husband had dubbed the *Revenge* was now ready to accommodate seventy fighting men as a pirate ship.

The sun had not yet risen one morning in late June of 1717 when a carriage pulled up at the dock, and the black driver leaped down to take off two small trunks. He held out an arm to assist his passenger. The man who dismounted might have been attired for a fancy-dress ball. He wore a rakish black felt hat, a full-sleeved shirt, a brace of pistols and a cape. His black boots gleamed in the lantern light. The servant lifted two trunks into a small boat. There was a gentle splash as it pushed off, and soon all that was visible was a dark shape in the stern as the small craft slid quietly through the water.

Aboard the *Revenge* it was soon apparent to the crew that their captain, with his ruffled shirt front and lace at the wrists, was something of a dandy and no seafaring man at all. Luckily for the major, the experienced Israel Morton had looked out for his interests. The quartermaster had screened all members of the crew before hiring them to be sure that they were the sort of men who would turn pirate given the opportunity. Now he watched as Bonnet stood before the crew assembled on deck.

The major was unaware that he presented an almost comic figure as he raised his ruffled fist and shouted, "From now on this is a pirate ship, men, and I expect you to take every damned vessel we can find."

"Every red-blooded man who will join us in getting rich, step forward," put in the quartermaster fiercely. Morton had confided to key men in the crew that he was prepared to break a few heads if any of the men showed opposition, but that proved unnecessary. The entire crew stepped forward. He had chosen well.

On their part, the men were filled with excitement. As was the habit of pirates, they set about electing their own officers. They voted in Morton formally as quartermaster, and with his urging, the swashbuckling Bonnet as captain. Later that day they voted on the pirates' Articles of Agreement.

Now Stede Bonnet paced the deck in great elation. In a few days he would show the crew what sort of captain he was! And he did. He began to order the quartermaster to tie men to the mast and lash them for breaking minor rules. A more serious infraction elicited the terrible penalty of marooning. With deceptive gentleness he would go up to the offending seaman and say, "I shall make you governor of the next deserted island we see!" Struggling and protesting, the seaman would be forcibly put off the ship at that island and left to die.

For a while the luck of this "gentleman" turned pirate was phenomenal, and his reputation for cruelty became so widespread that the reward for his capture exceeded even that of Blackbeard. It is said that despite the tales told of pirate horrors, Stede Bonnet was the only buccaneer who actually made his prisoners walk the plank.

Off the Virginia Capes Bonnet came upon the *Anne* from Glasgow, Scotland, and the *Turbet* from Barbados and seized them both. The latter vessel was unfortunate to have come from Bonnet's home port, for he ordered her burned to the waterline to keep word of his activities from reaching home. Although the seamen of a captured ship were usually offered the opportunity to join the pirates, there is no record of the fate of the crew of the *Turbet*.

The next vessels to be captured by Bonnet were two English ships, the *Endeavor* out of Bristol and the *Young* of Leith. Then he headed for South Carolina and Charles Towne, where the sea trade was heavy and the riches to be obtained by looting were enormous. On the way he captured a brigantine from New England and a sloop from Barbados.

Now his ship needed cleaning, for her sides and bottom were heavy with barnacles. Morton found a suitable location, and the crew went to work right away. Careening a ship was a dangerous task that had to be done quickly—ideally in less than forty-eight hours—for a ship on its side was highly vulnerable. The cleaning safely completed, the pirates took a vote on where they should sail next.

Then the men of the *Revenge* made a bold move. They voted to head for the Spanish Main—the northern coast of Colombia and Venezuela—and gold. It was a fateful decision.

Bonnet had been back at sea for only a day or two when he met another pirate ship. It was customary for pirate captains who were friends to fire cannon salvos to greet each other when they met. In this case, however, the pirates had never met, and civilities were exchanged instead. Bonnet stood staring across at the other ship, uncommonly impressed at the sight of the huge, broad-shouldered, ferocious fellow leaning against the rail eyeing him through binoculars.

Although most men of the day were clean-shaven, this man's face, up to the eyes, was submerged in a black beard of the most extravagant length. He was dressed in black with a broad-brimmed hat, knee boots, and a veritable arsenal of pistols hung from a sling over his shoulder. The broad belt around the man's waist held more pistols and daggers along with an immense cutlass.

Stede Bonnet recognized this man with considerable shock. He was facing the most awesome member of the Brethren of the Coast, Captain Edward Teach—or Blackbeard, as many called him.

Blackbeard invited Captain Bonnet over to his ship, plied him with drink, and then suggested that they join forces. He made the point that two pirate ships, working together to stalk and overtake their prey, were more efficient than one. Bonnet, believing that Blackbeard must be impressed by his reputation, accepted the invitation, and the two vessels continued on their way in quest of gold. Between Guadaloupe and the Virgin Islands, they seized several ships loaded with valuable cargo.

But as they maneuvered, closed in, attacked, and boarded the ships together, Blackbeard became contemptuous of Bonnet, quickly seeing him as a man who had no skills in handling either a ship or a crew. Captain Teach knew of several methods to dispose of this liability.

After inviting Bonnet on board for a dinner where liquor flowed copiously, Blackbeard warmly patted his friend on the shoulder and told him that the luxurious quarters on *his* ship would be far more suitable for a man of Bonnet's standing and gentlemanly background. Blackbeard suggested that if a rougher sort of fellow from his own ship, such as

Lieutenant Turner, took over the captaincy of Bonnet's ship, it would result in a more lucrative arrangement for all. A liquor-befuddled Bonnet agreed, and the next day Bonnet's crew voted for Turner to replace him as their captain.

There were still two pirate ships, but now there was only *one* crew, and over it, one commander: Blackbeard. Communication with other vessels was swift, and the news of what had happened was shouted across the water from ship to passing ship until Bonnet's humiliation was the joke of the coast.

The career of the man who would a-pirating go had received a severe setback. He still came and went as he pleased but made no decisions, seldom joining the men in their pleasures ashore. He spent his days reading and brooding. It was obvious to him as to everyone that Blackbeard had no intention of assigning him any responsibility.

For a time, Stede Bonnet saw his folly and was full of shame when he thought of what he had done as a pirate. If this insight had been lasting and if true repentance had occurred, Bonnet's future might have been very different; however, his chagrin was only a symptom of his natural inclination to sulk when frustrated.

Now Blackbeard, loaded with loot, cast about for ways of eliminating men who would normally share it. Turner rejoined Blackbeard, who instructed Bonnet to return to his ship and go into Bath Town to surrender to Governor Eden and receive the king's pardon.

"I will rejoin you soon and do the same. Then we will divvy up the loot," Blackbeard promised him.

Major Bonnet went to Bath Town and was absolved of all his deeds by the governor, but Blackbeard never appeared. In fact, he did not even approach Bath at all but sailed away, and a furious Bonnet never laid eyes on the loot or his "friend" again.

Shortly afterward, the pardoned Stede Bonnet was seen no more in Bath Town and a "Captain Edwards" appeared on the deck of the *Revenge*, sailing north upon the high seas. Bonnet thought his new name would conceal his identity and someday even enable him to go back to Barbados as Stede Bonnet. Later, he changed his name again, dubbing himself Captain Thomas—perhaps for his grandfather and uncle, who were both named Thomas.

In July 1718 Bonnet anchored the *Revenge* off Cape Henlopen, Delaware, and shortly after nine that evening he and his crew were delighted to see a large ship drop anchor in fourteen fathoms of water at the mouth of the river. "Captain Thomas" sent five men hurrying off in a rowboat to seize the stranger.

The mate on the deck of the *Francis*, who would be well able to testify later, described what happened: "I saw men approaching in what seemed to be a canoe, and I thought they were probably friendly. I called out to them saying, 'Where are you from?' One of them hollered back, 'Captain Thomas Richards from St. Thomas and Captain Read from Philadelphia.' Then he asked, 'Where are you from?' I answered, 'Antigua. You are welcome to come aboard,' and I had a man lower a rope to them."

As soon as the strangers came aboard they clapped their hands to their cutlasses and roughly shouted, "You are taken!"

The pirates then forced the *Francis*, along with the *Fortune*, which they had seized the day before, to sail with them out of Delaware Bay and south toward the Carolinas.

"Captain Thomas" was in high spirits. Although still angry about Blackbeard's trick, he was regaining his confidence and reveling in his success at his newly resumed career.

"Gold is gold no matter how you've got it," he had always said, "whether by privateering or piracy." He looked years younger now than when he had left Blackbeard and sailed into Bath Town. He was a man for whom excitement was the breath of life and danger an intoxicating stimulant racing through his veins. He relished the discovery of each new vessel and the attack. He also prided himself on being a much more experienced seaman than on that early morning when he left Barbados in his first ship.

Today he took the wheel himself and with his two prizes, the *Francis* and the *Fortune*, sailing on either side, he pictured himself lining his pockets with gold. It did not occur to him, as he sailed out of Delaware Bay, his men carousing and guzzling rum punch, that he was about to make the worst decision of his career.

Since the *Revenge* was entirely too well known as a pirate vessel, "Captain Thomas" now renamed her the *Royal James*. She had not been cleaned in some time, and Bonnet had to find a place to careen her. As luck would have it, she was also leaking, and repairs would add to the time the vessel was helpless.

Arriving at the mouth of the Cape Fear River, the pirates decided to sail upriver to an isolated cove and careen the sloop. If Bonnet had been as experienced as he thought he was, he simply would have changed to one of the two captured vessels with "clean heels." Both were in better condition than the *Royal James*.

As Bonnet's crew worked, citizens a little farther south were girding themselves against new pirate attacks. Of the southern ports that had been victimized by pirates, Charles Towne had suffered more than most. The vicious Captain Charles Vane had terrorized Charlestonians, and not long afterward Blackbeard had audaciously laid siege to the city. Now there was word that Captain Vane had returned! In fact, he had sacked a small vessel from Antigua right in sight of Charles Towne harbor.

Before releasing the crews on these ships, Vane had slyly hinted that he was planning to sail south, put in at one of the rivers and stay on in the area. This was a ruse to delay any vessels that might set out after him, for Vane was actually going to leave immediately and sail northward. The misinformation had been carried to Colonel William Rhett, who was ready to give hot pursuit.

Meanwhile the *Royal James* was still attending to maintenance. Cleaning and repairs had taken much longer than Bonnet had estimated. Life as a buccaneer had its drawbacks. One was being unable to seek parts and repairs in a harbor that offered these services to law-abiding vessels. Quartermaster Morton had gone to scout for what he needed in Charles Towne. It was not easy to find replacement parts, and the pirates had to capture a small ship in the river and salvage what they needed. The prisoners they released went to Charles Towne and reported that pirates were careening in the Cape Fear.

Everyone hearing this news was convinced the pirates were Captain Vane and his crew. But before Colonel Rhett went up the Cape Fear he took advantage of a wind from the north and sailed southward, thinking Vane might already be on his way. Of course, there was no sign of him, since the wily captain had headed north. Colonel Rhett now slowly sailed up the Cape Fear in search of the careened pirate ship.

Suddenly, he saw his pirates ahead—not one but three ships lying at anchor near a spit of land. In their eagerness to reach them the pilots of both Rhett's ships ran aground in shallow water. There was no way to get back afloat until high tide. It was too late that night to approach the ships more closely.

By now the pirates had seen the masts of Rhett's ships, and their first impulse was to set out by night to capture them. But what they saw, after paddling through the water in the darkness, was not the unarmed vessels they expected but rather sixteen mounted guns on two large sloops. They scurried back to report to Bonnet.

That night Stede Bonnet prepared for battle, transferring all arms and prisoners to his ship and abandoning the other two. At daylight when he made a run for it, Rhett's two sloops headed toward him, hoping to board. Colonel Rhett was flushed with excitement, believing that Charles Vane, who had all of Charles Towne aroused, was within his grasp. He could see himself returning with the notorious pirate captain as his prisoner.

Bonnet sailed sidelong toward shore and grounded his ship. Now it was impossible for Colonel Rhett to keep the *Royal James* between his ships, and the result was that both the *Henry* and the *Sea Nymph* also ran aground—but not in quite the position Rhett would have chosen. They were parallel to the *Royal James*, and both were in gunshot range.

As the tide began to fall, the pirate ship listed to port, providing cover for the pirates to shoot from behind the starboard rail, while Rhett's vessel listed toward the *Royal James*, exposing the men on Colonel Rhett's deck to devastating gunfire from the outlaws.

The firing continued six hours. Neither side was able to use cannon, for Bonnet's cannon were aimed toward the sky and Rhett's were aimed toward the water. At last the *Henry* floated free and began to move toward the pirate vessel. Bonnet shouted over the speaking trumpet, "Stay where you are. I'm sending a flag of truce aboard you." Rhett was enraged that they thought he would surrender.

The truce party boarded, and Colonel Rhett could hardly conceal his surprise when he found that the pirate captain did not ask for his capitulation but wanted to surrender to *him*. Dazed, Rhett accepted as Bonnet surrendered himself, his ship and his crew.

Rhett had an even greater shock in store for him. He now realized that his captive was not Charles Vane! The prisoners from the two ships the pirate had captured immediately identified him as the infamous Captain Stede Bonnet. Rhett took him prisoner and delivered him to Charles Towne.

In that gracious port city, Bonnet's treatment was most courteous, and he and two of his men were even placed under arrest at the marshal's home rather than the prison. Yet the fact that he would have to stand trial, even though the death penalty was not expected, so enraged Bonnet that he and one of the crewmen, dressed in women's clothes, escaped and set out northward in a small open boat. They had little food or water. The weather suddenly became stormy, and the pair was forced to turn back to Sullivan's Island. Here Rhett captured Bonnet again, and this time the attitude of the authorities toward the pirate captain was harsh. He had forfeited the sympathy some Charlestonians had previously held for him as a "gentleman."

His own men testified to the ships he had taken and his crimes. They were later hanged, and a jury found Bonnet "guilty as charged."

Even a desperate letter in which Bonnet pleaded his new conversion to Christianity did not move Governor Johnson, who well remembered that Stede Bonnet had the blood on his hands of numerous other murders in addition to those that had convicted him. Nor did Johnson forget that on an earlier foray into the Charles Towne harbor Bonnet had threatened death and destruction to the city. The escape attempt only confirmed that the pirate couldn't be trusted.

In his letter to the governor, Bonnet nevertheless begged to be made even a menial servant to His Honor and asked that his life be spared for "the reputation of my family." Ironically, he had not communicated with that family since he had left Barbados.

Wednesday, December 10, was set as the day of execution. From the time Major Bonnet, dressed in his lace-trimmed clothes, had stepped into the boat at the Barbados dock until the tenth of December of 1718 his life of excitement, danger, bloodshed and violence had lasted only a little over a year. As one once favored with wealth, the company of the best society on Barbados and the respect of his friends, he now seemed a rebel without a cause.

As the time for his execution approached, Bonnet was in such a state of terror that he could neither sleep nor eat. The prospect of death unnerved him. The appointed day dawned clear and sunny. Outside the watch house where he was imprisoned, Stede Bonnet could hear a steadily increasing roar of voices. A crowd was gathering. The hanging of a pirate was a public holiday, and entire families came from the countryside around to make a day of it. He heard the voices of hawkers selling food and drink. But the dreaded sound was yet to come. He knew what it would be like, for he had heard it each time one of his men was taken away. He waited with apprehension. Then the creaking wheels were there. It was the hanging cart, come for him.

A crescendo of shouts rose from the crowd: "Get him. Bring him out!"

He heard the scrape of the jailer's boots on the stone floor approaching his cell. He couldn't make his legs work, and two smelly, burly men grabbed him roughly, carrying him along, his feet barely touching the ground. They hoisted him into the vehicle. He thought it would take him straight to the gallows, but instead the horse drawing the cart turned in the opposite direction.

The route was to be a circuitous one, turning down several Charles Towne streets so the assembled crowd could see him pass. Boys followed the cart, thrusting their jeering faces up at his. Some spat upon him. In all his dreams of glory he had never anticipated this! Suddenly a little girl ran up to the cart and thrust a bouquet of wildflowers in his hands. Her mother jerked her back.

When the horse and cart finally drew up at the gallows, the crowd became quiet, eagerly awaiting his last words. Mouth dry, he opened his lips to speak, but no words came. The crowd waited. Would it be something impudent, some unrepentant statement, or a word of warning to the men in the crowd on the folly of becoming a pirate? These people would be hard to surprise. They had heard it all from other pirates.

Bonnet's entire body was trembling as if with ague. He opened his mouth a second time, but no words came. Now the people let out a roar of contempt and disappointment. To hear a man's last words before he died was one of the most thrilling parts of a hanging, but all Captain Stede Bonnet could do was sit in the cart shaking, unable to speak a word! Urchins shouted insults and hurled pieces of discarded food at him, hoping to get some response. None came.

The cart moved forward toward the gallows, and Bonnet looked up numbly at the dark noose silhouetted against the blue South Carolina sky. For the first time he spoke. "Oh my God, oh my God," he repeated over and over.

The hangman placed the noose around his neck. He heard the crack of a whip on the horse's rump. The cart jolted out from under him, and with a searing collar of pain around his throat Stede Bonnet felt himself hanging in midair.

As he writhed in the torment that followed, there were seconds when the past streamed through Bonnet's brain—rides down lush green avenues of tropical plants . . . shaded plantation house rooms . . . the burning heat of the sun in the blue sky . . . family faces . . . everything gone now in a nightmare of agony and slow death at the end of the hangman's rope miles from home. Brightly colored fireworks burst behind his eyes, sparks soaring, flying, falling, fading into eternal night.

Even after his death convulsions ceased, the captain's manacled hands clutched a tiny bouquet of flowers. Then the fingers relaxed. Israel Morton stepped quickly forward, picked the bouquet up and melted back into the crowd.

The "Gentleman Pirate" was no more. His body would be left hanging there for four days.

Cleland House

from *Ghosts of Georgetown*
by Elizabeth Robertson Huntsinger

A tragic wedding day left the ghost that now haunts the Cleland House. It is the ghost of a woman whose death was a terrible accident, conceived by no one and executed by what had appeared to be a beautiful and exquisite wedding gift.

Anne Withers lived with her parents on the Georgetown waterfront during the prosperous years preceding the Civil War. Her father was a socially prominent rice planter. Desiring to keep his family involved in Georgetown society, they lived most of the year in their Front Street townhouse.

Built in 1737, their comfortable home was reputed to be the oldest home in Georgetown. It was located near the point where St. James Street met the Sampit River.

The Cleland House originally faced the river. In 1730s Georgetown, Front Street was a secondary thoroughfare, so the rear of the home faced the road.

For thirty years, a chimney on each end of the house provided warmth against the cold winter and the perpetual dampness of the river. In 1767, one room was added at each end of the house, enclosing the chimneys.

The Cleland House already had a great deal of history behind it before it was occupied by the Withers family.

Many prominent guests had stayed in the home. During the Revolutionary War, Baron von Steuben and Baron deKalb were reputed to have been guests in the house while traveling with General Lafayette. Aaron Burr slept there preceding one of his visits to the Oaks Plantation, where his daughter, Theodosia, lived. The Withers family was quite proud of the history of their house.

When Anne fell in love with a handsome sea captain, her father was a bit displeased but not very surprised. After all, the girl was raised beside the waterfront and she grew up intensely interested in the comings and goings of the tall-masted ships.

Anne's father hoped his pretty daughter would marry the son of another planter, but he had to admit that this sea captain was not bad at all. The fellow was quite wealthy, as well as being very handsome. He and Anne would have good-looking children.

Anne's parents, after being informed of the couple's desire to wed, gave their consent to the marriage. With their parents' blessings they went ahead with plans for the nuptials.

The wedding was scheduled to take place when the sea captain returned from his next voyage. The pair would marry downstairs in the Cleland House, with a reception in the ornate garden behind the home.

Anne was delighted but she prepared for her wedding with nervous anticipation. What if his ship was caught in a storm or stranded in the doldrums? What if he did not arrive for the wedding day?

The months flew by and, much to Anne's relief, her captain arrived in Georgetown, well and safe, a week before their wedding day.

One night, while catching his breath amidst the flurry of parties and social engagements that preceded the nuptials, the captain told Anne he had brought her a wedding present.

He reached in his pocket and brought out the gift, wrapped loosely in a linen handkerchief. As the material unfolded in his hand, a glittering gold bracelet appeared.

Anne gave an exclamation of delight and awe. In all her life she had never seen such a treasure.

The bracelet in her captain's hand was a chain of linked gold beetles.

Each tiny creature had glistening gem eyes. They were perfectly lifelike, except for their gold countenance and lack of legs. Never, except in nature, had Anne seen beings of such flawless perfection. The beetles wrought in solid gold apparently had a foreign origin, for Anne had never seen insects quite like these around Georgetown.

As if he could read Anne's thoughts, her fiancé said, "It came from Egypt. The old trader I bought it from assured me it is a rare antiquity found in the tomb of an Egyptian princess."

As he struggled to undo the clasp to put the bracelet on Anne's wrist, the captain went on, "No doubt it's very old and of rare quality, but I don't know about the Egyptian princess part. That sounds wonderfully mysterious, but the trader was a superstitious old sod, reeking of whiskey. He said he'd had nothing but bad luck since he bought this fine piece off a blind beggar."

When the clasp still would not come undone, Anne finally withdrew her wrist. "Don't try anymore," she told her captain. "I won't wear it until our wedding. The clasp has probably not been worked in many years. My maid will get it open, even if she has to oil it and pry it loose."

When Anne returned to her room, she gave the bracelet to her maid and asked her to undo the clasp. She did not see the bracelet again until her wedding hour, several days later.

When the hour came for her to dress in her bridal finery, Anne found the bracelet laid along with all her other carefully chosen attire. When Anne was dressed, her maid gently fastened the glistening circlet of beetles around her wrist.

Anne turned her wrist this way and that, causing the bright stone eyes of the gold beetles to wink and glitter. What an extraordinarily lovely bracelet, she thought.

"It's time, Miss Anne," her maid advised the bride.

Anne stood up, gave her maid a hug, and walked out her bedroom door. The time had come to descend the stairs to the flower-festooned parlor where she would marry her captain. All her family and close friends were awaiting her descent.

Anne felt a tug of apprehension as she approached the staircase. This was such an important moment, the most serious, most happy moment of her life—and this bracelet was starting to itch, starting to prickle, starting to prick her. . . .

Anne's maid heard a terrible scream tear from her mistress's throat.

She dashed out of Anne's bedroom and into the upstairs hall to find Anne collapsed at the top of the stairs.

The bride was deathly pale in all her shimmering white finery. The only color on her ghostly alabaster form came from the gleaming red eyes of the golden beetles, and the blood that ran from the points where each beetle clung to her wrist.

Anne's maid tore at the bracelet as wedding guests ran up the stairs.

She gasped in horror as the bracelet finally gave way, the previously hidden legs of the beetles now wrenched loose from her mistress's tender flesh. However, it was too late. Anne was already dead.

Anne's parents were overcome with shock and grief. Her fiancé could not forgive himself for giving his love such an unspeakably horrible present.

He immediately set sail for London, the bracelet locked away in a wooden box in his cabin.

The captain took the bracelet to the finest chemist in all London to have its structure and content analyzed. The chemist explained that the bracelet, perhaps never worn, was designed by the ancient Egyptians as a device to punish grave robbers. Each beetle had minute, sharp legs which held poison. These legs were hidden in the beetle's body and ingeniously designed to deploy only when warmed by body heat.

After Anne had worn the bracelet for a short time, every needle-like leg came down and punctured the tender flesh of her wrist, poisoning her instantly.

Poor Anne died in terror, with no idea what was happening to her. She was aware only of the excruciating pain of thirteen fiery-eyed beetles digging into her wrist just as she was descending into the misty dream of her wedding.

Since that day, Anne has been seen many times in the garden behind her house. Some say the reason why Anne Withers occasionally comes back to her home by the river is the inexplicable terror of her death. She still does not understand what terrible force snatched her life away at its most joyous moment. Some nights, when the moon is nearly full and the river warms the cool breeze that blows in from the ocean, she can be seen in all her antebellum bridal finery walking through the back garden. And those who have seen her walking there will tell you that the look of bewilderment on her face reveals that she is wondering what went so horribly wrong on her wedding day long ago.

The Georgia Werewolf

from *Georgia Ghosts*
by Nancy Roberts

Even today, Talbot County, located between Macon and Columbus, is a lonely, heavily wooded part of the state. In the nineteenth century, the county was even more remote and undeveloped, yet it served as a home to some of the state's elite society. One of the most elite of Talbot County's families was the Burt family.

In the 1840s, the Burt family was a highly respected part of the community and sufficiently well off to enjoy European travel and other luxuries reserved for the wealthy. Mildred Owen Burt was widowed at thirty-seven. Her inheritance included sixteen slaves, sheep, hogs, cattle, two horses, a large assortment of books, a barouche carriage, and a brace of fine pistols (she was an excellent markswoman).

Mrs. Burt loved to read, but of her four children—Joel, Sarah, Emily Isabella, and Mildred—only Isabella was as fond of reading as her mother. Isabella particularly enjoyed the books on the supernatural which her mother brought back from Europe.

Isabella's unusual appearance may have driven her toward the quiet solitude of the world of books. Sarah and Mildred were passably pretty and resembled their mother, but Isabella had inherited some of her father's characteristics. He had been a handsome man, though somehow his thick, dark hair, heavy brows, large brown eyes, and tall frame gave him a sinister appearance. However, whenever the curve of his lips parted to reveal a generous smile enhanced by white teeth, any trace of the sinister disappeared. Isabella's hair was thick and dark, like her father's, but shaggier. Her dense brows covered eyes that were smaller than her father's, while her teeth, revealed during rare smiles, were pointed, as if they had been shaped with a file.

On one trip to the dentist, Isabella's mother asked the man if something could be done to improve the appearance of Isabella's teeth, perhaps by blunting them. The dentist, not a particularly sensitive man, disregarded this suggestion. "Her teeth are perfectly healthy," he said. "After all, aren't we humans basically carnivores?" Mrs. Burt was too irritated to reply.

It was not long after that trip to the dentist that Isabella fell ill. The only substance that seemed to ease her restless nocturnal tossing was a syrup containing opium. Isabella quickly grew dependent on the syrup, often rising from her bed at night in search of the drug. Many a night the family heard her moaning in pain and addiction. Some nights, even the syrup would not ease her insomnia, and she took to roaming the surrounding countryside.

During the long afternoons of December and January, Isabella spent much of her time reading in the family library. In a sense, the girl's invalidism and solitude eased her mother's mind, for at least Mrs. Burt did not have to worry that she would elope or become involved with a young man of the wrong class. The same could not be said for her other two daughters. In fact, Sarah had become involved with a young man named William Gorman. Though Gorman was heir to his father's farm, Mrs. Burt was concerned that the young man seemed more interested in mining for gold than in becoming a gentleman farmer. Mildred was away at school for the winter, as was Joel, so Mrs. Burt did not have the opportunity to worry about Mildred and Joel quite as often.

One February morning, Gorman stopped by the Burt house with a strange piece of news. During the night, some of the Gorman family's sheep had been attacked. Their shepherd denied having been asleep.

The news greatly distressed Sarah and Mrs. Burt, for they realized their own sheep might also be in danger. However, Isabella simply looked up from her book and asked if the shepherd had seen anything among the herd.

"He says he saw no panther or bear among them," Gorman replied.

"Nor anything else?" persisted Isabella.

"Not that I know of. What do you mean?" asked Gorman.

"Perhaps a wolf?"

"We have very few wolves around here. And a wolf could not attack the sheep without our dogs catching the animal's odor and barking," said Gorman. "That would alert the shepherd immediately."

"What would the shepherd do then?" asked Isabella.

"Frighten it away, or kill it," said Gorman.

Isabella seemed to pause for a moment and consider Gorman's response. Finally she commented, "Well, every animal feeds upon another."

Gorman was now irritated with the young girl, though determined not to show it. "This attack was not for food," he said sharply. Then, changing the subject, he inquired, "Mrs. Burt, I am on my way to the store. Do you need anything?"

"I don't think so, but it is very kind of you to inquire, William."

"Mother, it would be nice to bake some lemon tarts," said Sarah. "If you would like for me to make them, then we need some lemons." She looked at her mother. "And some fine-ground white flour for the crust," she continued.

"Of course I would," said Mrs. Burt. "Ask the store to put it on my bill, William. Four lemons and five pounds of flour."

Later that night, Sarah heard William return from the store and rushed out to the porch to meet him. Mrs. Burt noticed that the two talked on the porch for at least a quarter of an hour before Sarah entered the front door, groceries in hand. That was entirely too long for those two to be alone together, Mrs. Burt thought. Mrs. Burt then heard Sarah speaking with Isabella. Though Mrs. Burt could not hear Isabella's question, she did hear Sarah's reply.

"Yes. They have found out more, Isabella," Sarah said. "But I don't want to talk about it. It's horrible!"

Mrs. Burt then retired to her room. She walked over to the window and stared out thoughtfully. By now, the men must be making plans to lie in wait for the marauder, she thought, whatever or whoever it was. She knew they would form a posse and shoot it.

On Friday afternoon, two days later, Gorman came by the Burt house again. Sarah had made the lemon tarts that afternoon, and he stayed long enough to join them in a tart and a cup of tea. Isabella persisted in asking him for more news about the animal that had attacked the sheep. He replied that there had been no more attacks on the sheep, but that "something happened at a nearby cattle farm." The news elicited a torrent of questions from the excited young girl.

"Why do you want to talk so much about anything so unpleasant, Isabella?" asked Sarah.

Isabella turned on her sister with fury in her eyes. "You know nothing about it!" she shouted. Then, to everyone's surprise, she grabbed Sarah's plump arm and jerked her violently.

"Isabella, release your sister at once!" Mrs. Burt screamed. Isabella dropped Sarah's arm, but her face was dark with anger.

Gorman made no comment. He thanked Mrs. Burt for her hospitality, said something to Sarah in a low tone, and left. As soon as he was gone, Mrs. Burt said, "Sarah, get the account books. I want to go over our inventory of sheep, hogs, and cattle. We must check each week and make certain all are accounted for. We will start tomorrow matching the figures to your father's will."

A moment later there was a knock at the front door.

"I'll answer it," cried Sarah, jumping up and rushing to the door. Mrs. Burt briefly heard Gorman's voice, then Sarah quickly stepped out on the porch and closed the front door behind her. Why had William come back so quickly? thought Mrs. Burt.

Out on the porch, Gorman spoke to Sarah in grave tones. "We are going to try to solve this problem tonight, Sarah, even if we must use silver bullets to shoot this creature," he stated. "I wanted to leave this little pistol with you for an emergency. Please do not go outdoors during the night."

"Oh, I'm sure I'm in no danger, William. I don't want *you* to get hurt!"

"We shall kill the creature, Sarah, if we can get close enough. I will drop by the house tomorrow to tell you what happened." Gorman then gave Sarah a brief hug and hurried off.

When Sarah returned to the kitchen, she found her mother and Isabella preparing supper. Sarah felt a strange tension in the air. Not long after their meal, Isabella excused herself. Mrs. Burt went up to her bedroom next, and Sarah also retired earlier than usual. We all must be more upset by this than we will admit, thought Sarah, trying to explain the tension she felt earlier.

Just after midnight, Sarah was awakened by a strange sound. She hurriedly put on her robe and shoes and eased open the door. No one was in the hall, but two figures were on the stairs. She could see her mother standing perfectly still, concealing herself by the curve of the rail just above the first-floor landing. As Sarah looked past her mother, she saw Isabella slipping out the front door. Her mother soon followed.

Sarah assumed Isabella was simply wandering outside, as she often did when she couldn't sleep. But why had her mother followed? Surely, they both were aware of the danger posed by the mysterious animal roaming the countryside. Determined to find out what was going on, Sarah grabbed the pistol Gorman had left her and followed the pair from a safe distance.

Once outside, Sarah could see that the two—her mother following Isabella at a discrete distance—were headed toward the winter sheep pasture. Sarah could see Mrs. Burt close in upon her daughter, just as it seemed Isabella was preparing to spring upon one of the sheep. Then she heard the animal's terrified cry. Mrs. Burt shouted at Isabella. The girl spun around and rushed toward her mother with a howl of rage. As Isabella turned, Sarah could see there was a knife in her hand. Sarah was close enough to shoot but could not point the gun at her own sister. Isabella was almost upon her mother when a shot rang out across the pasture. At that moment, Sarah fainted.

The next morning, she awoke to find herself in her own bed. The doctor was bending over her. "I thought I had better check on you again, young lady, just to be sure you were all right," he said.

"What happened?" Sarah mumbled.

"Young Gorman came for me in the middle of the night. It seems he was heading a posse of men hunting a werewolf, and your sister Isabella somehow got herself into the middle of it. She's in bed, too. When she wakes up from the dose of morphine I gave her, she's going to be in real pain. One of the men shot off her left hand. She's just lucky the bullet didn't hit her in the heart."

At that moment, a sense of awareness dawned on Sarah, though she couldn't quite verbalize what she knew in her heart. Then she remembered her mother. "Mother. How is she?" she asked.

"Mrs. Burt? Why, she's doing fine," the doctor replied. "Has a powder burn on her right hand, that's all. She said she heard a noise outside, got her pistol, and was on her way to investigate when she stumbled. The pistol she was carrying must have gone off accidentally. Women don't know how to handle guns."

This last statement struck Sarah, for her mother was known as an excellent markswoman. She did not contradict the doctor, though she knew there was no way that gun could have gone off accidentally.

As soon as Isabella's wound had healed, Mrs. Burt sent her youngest daughter to "visit a relative in Paris." Only Mrs. Burt knew the girl was really being sent to Paris to be treated by a famous specialist. The doctor's field was lycanthropy—a psychological disease in which an emotionally disturbed person manages to convince themselves they have become a werewolf.

Some months later, Isabella came home. While she was away, there were no more problems with the local livestock. Some say a minor incident or two did happen after she returned, but these rumors were never proven. "Miss Isabella," as she came to be known, never married. Despite the persistent rumors she was a werewolf, she lived in the county her whole life and managed to avoid serious persecution due to the prominence of her family.

Mrs. Mildred Owen Burt was seventy-eight when she died in 1890. Some years later, Isabella died. Her body is said to be buried on sacred ground in a Talbot County cemetery. Those who live near the cemetery believe her diseased, disordered spirit still roams the land, moaning and howling in the night. All we really know is that somewhere in the vast, undeveloped land of Talbot County, there is a grave containing the body of the only woman in Georgia reputed to be a werewolf.

Pawleys Island Terriers

from *More Ghosts of Georgetown*
by Elizabeth Robertson Huntsinger

Many summer visitors return to Pawleys Island year after year to enjoy the blissful ambiance of this diminutive South Carolina sea island linked to the mainland by two narrow causeways. Some have been making an annual pilgrimage since they were children, as their parents, grandparents, great-grandparents, and great-great-grandparents did before them.

For a century, two tiny dogs have returned summer after summer to frolic with happy abandon on the seashore of this four-mile-long, half-mile-wide island, where they spent their happiest hours. Devoted to each other in life, these little terriers who died long ago still cavort at the edge of the Atlantic. Often mistaken for lost dogs by those seeing them for the first time, they are well familiar to longtime residents, who know why the terriers appear for such a short time, then disappear without a trace.

Once the seasonal haven of antebellum rice planters, Pawleys Island saw an increase in summer visitors each decade after the Civil War. During the late 1800s, many Georgetonians spent a portion of the long, hot summer on Pawleys savoring the cool sea breeze coming off the Atlantic.

As the turn of the century neared, steamships stayed busy plying the Waccamaw River between Georgetown and the island, bringing boatloads of cheerful beachgoers from town as well as from other parts of the state. Most travelers from outside Georgetown journeyed into town by train and were taken from the station to the steamship dock by horse-drawn buggy. From there, they boarded the *Janie*, the *Ruth*, the *Madge*, the *Pelican*, or other local steamers. Often, the steamships were filled to capacity with island-bound passengers. Hearts soared and spirits lifted, for the travelers would soon be at Pawleys!

Though a number of families owned homes on the island and moved there for the summer, many visitors rented houses during the season. Still more stayed at seashore hotels and boardinghouses. Though the Ocean View Hotel and the Pawleys Island Hotel hosted many turn-of-the-century guests, perhaps the most popular destination was the Winyah Inn and the accompanying Winyah Inn Cottages, known simply as "Mrs. Butler's," after the hospitable owner and operator.

Once ensconced on the island, the summer people spent their days bathing in the ocean, fishing, shrimping, and crabbing. Their nights were filled with social and sporting activities. The evening itinerary at Mrs. Butler's during the first week of August 1898 included an oyster roast on Monday, a library party ending in a dance with live guitar and violin music on Tuesday, a literary and social night on Thursday, and a crabbing party on Friday. Dances were held at Mrs. Butler's and various island residences on Saturday night. In one such home, the lanterns had to be hung on hooks, since the force of so many people dancing caused lanterns placed on the mantels to vibrate onto the floor.

Other evenings were spent gigging flounder in the creek between the island and the mainland. Night gigging involved patiently plying a slow-moving rowboat as the light of a wood torch burning in a flat metal pan attached to the side of the boat illuminated the dark creek bottom. Sharp-pointed gig poles were poised expectantly above the water, waiting for the second that an elusive, flat-bodied flounder was spotted.

Lunches and suppers were usually highlighted by the fresh seafood that abounded. A typical menu at Mrs. Butler's consisted of an immense smorgasbord including turtle soup, oysters on the half shell, clam soup, and summer duck. Breakfast often featured a highly coveted delicacy: sea-turtle eggs. Morning beachcombers delighted in discovering the distinctive tracks of a mother loggerhead turtle and would follow the trail to the nest of precious eggs laid during the night. Before the eggs had a chance to mature and hatch, the nest would be robbed bare of its dozens of distinctively shaped eggs.

Many children were among the seasonal islanders. They stayed in summer homes or boardinghouses with their parents. A July 1897 edition of the *Georgetown Semi-Weekly Times* mentioned that there were twenty-five children staying at Mrs. Butler's.

In the family atmosphere that prevailed on the island, many youngsters were allowed to play in the sand and at the surf's edge with little supervision save that of older children. This carefree summer practice resulted in a near-tragedy that brought heartfelt praise and grateful attention to two heroic little turn-of-the-century terrier dogs.

One balmy Saturday afternoon, as the salty breeze cooled the blazing sand of the wide Pawleys Island beach, a group of children was busy just below the high-tide line digging and piling sand to construct an elaborate castle. Conditions were perfect. The tide was about halfway out, assuring that the castle would not be washed away before evening. Enough water was left in the sand from the high tide that, by digging the castle's moat deep enough, water would appear at the bottom of the trough. The sand was damp and easy to form into walls, bridges, and turrets.

The older children, more expert and serious about sand-castle construction than the younger ones, commanded the project. Smaller children were allowed to participate as serfs, following orders of where to dig, where to put more sand, and when to haul water for the moat.

The youngest was a cheerful toddler boy more interested in knocking over the older children's carefully constructed walls than in helping make them. It was the well-understood duty of the little boy's older siblings and companions that they were responsible for his safety when playing on the seashore. To keep him busy and to prevent him from destroying their growing sand castle, the older children gave the toddler a little bucket and shovel and persuaded him to dig in the sand on his own near where they were working.

Happy at first to have his own project, the little boy soon lost interest in digging and decided to wade into the surf and get some water in his bucket, as he had seen the older children do. Treading determinedly across the sloping beach toward the foamy tidal flow, he was unnoticed by the older children.

Never having walked in the pull and tug of the surf without his hand firmly held by someone larger, the little boy became unsteady on his feet as the outgoing water sucked the sand from under them. The receding tide and the heavier-than-usual surf soon combined to pull the toddler's feet out from under him. Within seconds, he was rolling helplessly. Despite the shallow depth of the water he was in, each outward roll of the surf pulled him several feet farther, until it seemed he would be lost in the ocean. An older person would have simply fought to sit up and then risen out of the rough surf, but the bewildered toddler was rolled like a piece of driftwood.

More than likely, no one would have ever been sure of his fate had not two terriers intervened. Mildly curious at the little boy's trek to the ocean's edge but razor-sharp alert as he lost his footing and fell, the dogs began barking furiously as he was rolled to and fro in the shallow surf. They rushed to the group of children working on the sand castle and barked with all their might. The children, familiar with the terriers, paid little attention until the wildly barking dogs ran into their midst, wrecking part of the castle. The youngsters leaped up, aghast at the destruction of their labor and surprised, too, for these terriers were not usually disruptive.

One of the older boys, his focus now averted from the sand castle, spied the toddler rolling helplessly in the surf. Crying out, he rushed to the water, followed by his playmates and the frantic terriers. The oldest children soon had him safely clasped. Realizing that the little boy could have been pulled out to sea without their knowledge was very sobering to the children, who had not known a care in the world just moments earlier. Overwhelmed with relief, they cuddled the toddler and praised and petted the terriers, which had ceased barking the second the child was out of the water. They now wriggled with delight, reveling in the attention they were receiving for their lifesaving deed.

A dance was held at one of the boardinghouses on the island that night. By the end of the evening, nearly everyone on Pawleys Island knew of the terriers' heroism.

No one was prouder than the lady who owned them. The male terrier and his smaller female mate were her greatest joy. She brought them along every summer to her family's house on the island. The family had several dogs, but the terriers were her favorites and her constant companions. She kept them impeccably bathed and groomed, fed them from the table, and talked to them as if they were human. She had spent many hours training them and positively reinforcing their good behavior, with the result that they were exceedingly obedient and well mannered. She included them in as many of her family's activities as was practical and safe. Disciplined and nurtured as intelligent, sensitive creatures, the terriers—as nearly all dogs will when treated so—developed intelligent, sensitive personalities.

Morning and evening, no matter what the weather, the lady walked her terriers along the shore. Although they had the freedom to leave the veranda of the family's oceanfront home, cross the high dunes, and romp on the beach at will, this did not equal the pleasure they took in their twice-daily walks with their mistress.

The terriers would race into and out of the shallow water, sometimes paddling seaward for a few minutes before making their way back to shore. There was no end to their delight as they romped with one another, snapping at the foam that always evaporated in their mouths and chasing the shorebirds that never failed to fly out of reach just in the nick of time. They never seemed to run out of energy as they pranced and played during these walks, showing off wildly for their beloved owner.

The day after the terriers saved the toddler, a hurricane swept the coast. It did not make landfall near Pawleys Island, but the gale-force winds, the raging rain, and the danger of hurricane-spawned tornadoes and waterspouts kept everyone on the island securely indoors for two days. The third day dawned with clear blue skies and a stiff breeze that seemed placid compared to the hurricane. At last, it was safe to frolic on the beach once more!

The mistress was delighted to finally have a stroll on the shore with her dogs. The terriers, friskier than ever after having been confined, gallivanted at the edge of the ocean, paddling out and back repeatedly, each time swimming a little farther.

While swimming toward shore, the male terrier was suddenly engulfed by a tremendous wave that came up behind him. Tired from his forays into the ocean, he was unprepared for this onslaught and was rolled under the wave. The fierce undertow then sucked his struggling little form back out, allowing him no chance to come to the surface for air.

Meanwhile, the other terrier did not bark but ran, tail tucked between her legs, up and down the hard-packed sand near the spot where she had last seen her mate. The mistress, fearing her pet was tiring, had been calling him in when the wave overtook him. When he did not surface after being engulfed, she became frantic. She, too, ran up and down the shore adjacent to where she had last seen the dog. Her eyes strained for a glimpse of his dark head, but he had disappeared.

After more than an hour, the lady returned sadly to her house, carrying the remaining terrier in her arms, for it refused to leave the shore on its own.

Late that afternoon, the lady crossed the sand dunes to walk along the ocean, as she did nearly every day. Only now, there was a lone terrier instead of a pair, and both mistress and dog were very sad indeed. Instead of frolicking on the shore, the terrier walked slowly and listlessly at her mistress's side, occasionally raising her head to gaze dolefully at the ocean.

All at once, the little creature was filled with energy. She raced across the shore to a dark mound partially covered in wet sand. The terrier dug rapidly and quickly unearthed the cold, wet form of her companion. When the lady caught up to the dog, the terrier was pulling her lifeless mate along the sand toward her mistress. Tears fell unchecked from the lady's eyes as she knelt to caress the wet, sandy fur. Slowly and sadly, she walked back to her house cradling the lifeless dog in her arms. She felt even worse for the remaining terrier, which barked happily and danced around her feet, thinking her mate was being brought home.

A pall fell over the entire family, which sent for a carpenter to build a tiny wooden box. The family lined it with soft blanket material before closing the little form away.

Rather than burying the terrier on the island, the family members took the coffin back to their plantation on the mainland, where they interred the little box in a quiet area of the garden. As the summer was nearly over, they decided not to return to Pawleys Island for the remainder of the season. This decision was not entirely for practical reasons. None of the family wanted to spend time so soon at the place where the cherished pet had died.

The surviving terrier suffered a worse bereavement than anyone in the family. Day and night, she whined and pawed the door until she was allowed outside, at which time she went straight to her companion's grave. The grieving dog could not be persuaded to leave the site, but had to be carried away no matter how long she had been sitting there. Nor could the dog be persuaded to eat. Despite all the love and tender care lavished upon her, she fell deeper into melancholy.

After less than two weeks, the lone terrier died, lying forlornly on the grave of her beloved mate. Another wooden box was made. Soon, there were twin graves in the garden. Petite marble stones were made to commemorate the final resting place of the two heroic dogs.

The following summer, the family made its annual move to Pawleys Island. Although everyone still missed the terriers, their quiet sadness had evolved into a wistful nostalgia. The terriers' mistress was now able to remember them with a smile rather than with tears.

Not long after the family's arrival, the nanny from a neighboring ocean-front house called on the mistress. She told the lady that her dogs were playing unattended on the beach. The nanny had been about to leave the shore with her young charges when the terriers had run down to the water near the delighted children. She had called the dogs but had not been able to get them to come back to the houses. Reaching the top of the dunes with the children, she had turned to call the dogs once more, but they were gone. Knowing that the lady would not want her dogs running loose, the nanny had come to tell her of their whereabouts.

The lady could not help smiling fondly at the description of the dogs. Appreciating the nanny's concern, she told her that these must be the pets of another, for hers had died nearly a year ago.

As the summer progressed, however, reports of her free-running terriers came to her from children who had played with the dogs during previous summers. These were the same dogs, the children innocently insisted, except that they played without barking and disappeared before they could be petted.

Still assuming the terriers in question belonged to another summer family, the lady began hoping to get a look at them. One evening, she was sitting atop the highest dune separating her home from the seashore, having just returned from the west veranda of her house, where she had watched a spectacular sunset over the creek with her family. She had just settled down on her high, sandy perch to view the twilight over the Atlantic when two dancing, prancing little creatures caught her eye where the surf met the hard-packed shore. Her terriers! Without another thought, she ran down the dune calling the dogs' names.

At the sound of her voice, the terriers stopped abruptly and pricked their ears. Then, in one motion, they bounded toward their mistress and ran in huge circles around her, pausing only to leap into the air and prance on their hind feet.

Arms held wide, the lady laughed out loud as the lively pair frolicked silently around her. When she was sure they must be exhausted and ready to lie down panting, they vanished! As far as she could see up and down the empty beach, no dogs were in view.

Many more times during the summers of her long life, the lady saw the terriers. Each visit was unexpected. She saw them by moonlight, in the heat of the afternoon, and in the misty early morning, but most often at twilight. Never was she able to touch them or hear their barks, but the dogs never failed to cause her heart to sing with joy. Fleeting as their appearances were, the dogs always appeared vibrant, alive, and exuberant.

Over the years, the lady and her family passed away. The house they summered in became the seasonal home of others who loved the island. The terriers, however, continued to frolic silently on the stretch of beach where they had once romped with their mistress and become heroes for saving the life of a helpless toddler.

Now, a century later, island residents who have heard the legend of the terriers know the fruitlessness of trying to catch these frisky creatures and return them to their owner. The phantom dogs and their mistress are occupants of another time in the genial history of Pawleys Island.

The Wagon of Death

from *The Hauntings of Williamsburg, Yorktown, and Jamestown*
by Jackie Eileen Behrend

Since Williamsburg was the capital of Virginia during most of the eighteenth century, any free person accused of a felony had to be tried in this city. During this period, there was little compromise in the judicial process. If a person was convicted of murder, arson, horse stealing, forgery, or piracy, he was often sentenced to hang. As a result, Williamsburg was the scene of numerous hangings.

If a person was sentenced to hang, it was thought that keeping him confined for a prolonged period of time was inhumane and cruel. Hanging was regarded a kinder punishment than imprisonment.

In the eighteenth century, this may have been the case. The conditions the inmates had to endure during their imprisonment were horrible. The cells were small, cramped, and unheated. The tiny barred windows contained no glass to protect the prisoners from the elements.

Prisoners slept on piles of insect-ridden straw. During later excavations of the prison grounds, heavy shackles were unearthed, providing evidence that prisoners were often chained to the floor.

Lice covered the walls. Roaches and rodents scurried throughout the cells. The smell alone was almost unbearable. Considering these conditions, death may have seemed a better option.

If found guilty of a heinous crime, the criminal was held in the overcrowded jail until the "Wagon of Death" came to escort him to the gallows. Long before this death wagon was in view, the condemned man could hear the creaking of the cart's wheels as it rolled down Nicholson Street. The prisoner was then forced to sit on his own coffin for the mile-long ride to Hangman's Road, knowing full well he would be inside the casket on his way back.

When the prisoner arrived at the gallows, he was usually the center of a social event. A public hanging brought people to the capital from all over the surrounding countryside. It was usually a festive, cheering crowd that greeted the prisoner when he arrived in the Wagon of Death.

A person can't help but feel a little sorry for the wayward criminals of the eighteenth century. We can only imagine the terror and panic they must have felt as they rode on the Wagon of Death, watching their last few minutes of life tick away.

The days of the hangman's rope are long gone. No physical evidence remains of the hangman's gallows on the outskirts of Williamsburg, but you can still visit the original Public Gaol, as it was called then.

The jail is one of the oldest buildings in the former capital city. It housed murderers, pirates, marauding Indians, runaway slaves, and common debtors until 1780, when Virginia's capital moved to Richmond. It continued to house offenders until 1910.

In addition to the jail, there have been other less tangible reminders of how we used to treat our criminals. For well over a century, haunting stories of the Wagon of Death have been reported. People living on Nicholson Street speak of hearing the sounds of a horse and wagon in the predawn hours. They dash to their windows, but they see nothing of this mysterious carriage or its ill-fated passengers.

James Daughtery, a guest at the spacious Coke-Garrett House in June 1985, told of an inexplicable incident he experienced early one morning while sleeping in one of the rooms facing Nicholson Street. He said, "I awoke to the sound of horses and the cracking of a whip. A loud gruff voice commanded the animals to move faster. I thought it was far too early for Colonial Williamsburg to have their horses on the street, but I knew I wasn't imagining what I was hearing. Then I remembered the myth of the Wagon of Death. I was determined to see if it really did exist. I ran to the window, but the street was empty of both horses and people. I was disappointed that I didn't see the death wagon for myself, but at least I knew I'd heard it."

Early one foggy morning in April 1992, Donald Reeves, a Colonial Williamsburg employee, had a similar experience. He was working in the Carpenter's Yard, then on Nicholson Street, preparing for a busy day of visitors. Donald said, "I was setting up the tool display in the shed when I heard the clacking of horses' hooves and the creaking of wagon wheels. I didn't think much of it until I realized it was so early, the sun hadn't risen yet. I still didn't pay much attention until I heard the sound of a whip cracking. Being an animal lover, I was upset thinking the horses were being mistreated. I ran outside but there wasn't anything there."

It would seem those living and working on Nicholson Street are not alone in their experiences. Tourists staying on Hangman's Road (now Capitol Landing Road) have heard the elusive horse and wagon as well. Kitty Miller was sleeping in a nearby hotel when she, too, was awakened by strange noises. Kitty is certain she heard "a horse whinny and the sound of a crowd cheering. I thought some event of Colonial Williamsburg's was going on outside. I couldn't believe they would be doing this so early in the morning, while people were trying to sleep. I was angry because I didn't sleep well the night before and I needed to get some rest. I went to the window to see what was going on, but the yard was empty! The sounds of the crowd just faded away."

To this day, no one has actually seen the legendary Wagon of Death or the horses that pull it. Most will agree, however, it not only exists but continues to pass down the historic streets of Williamsburg, as it has done for almost three centuries.

Milk and Candy

from *The Granny Curse and Other Ghosts and Legends from East Tennessee*
by Randy Russell and Janet Barnett

The frail woman was at the door again. And she was coming inside.

She came to Moody's store, located on the Childress Ferry Road in Sullivan County, at the same time every evening. She showed up just as he was closing shop. She was barefoot and pale of skin. Her dress was gray with age and wear, its hem ragged. The woman's hair was undone. It was long and dark. It hung loosely down her back.

She carried a chipped china teacup in one hand. It looked like one someone had thrown away.

"Milk, sir," she said, setting the cup on the counter. She placed a thick reddish coin next to it. The woman never really looked at him. She never looked at anything but the hard candy pieces in the large jars he kept on the counter.

He filled her broken cup with milk, as much as it would hold. When he brought it back to her, she pointed at the piece of candy she wanted this time. She had done this every day for five days now.

"I have a nice piece of ham and a bone I could let you have," Moody offered. "There's a bit of cornmeal that's left over. I could give you that if you wanted. You could pay me at the end of summer, if you would like."

The frail woman was too skinny to be alive, he thought.

She shook her head at his offers and pointed at the piece of candy she wanted. Moody removed the jar lid and watched her slide her hand in to pick out one piece of candy. She never took two.

The woman left with her piece of candy and two ounces of milk. It was the same every time.

"You might as well face it," Moody's wife said. "She's a ghost."

"Her money's real enough," Moody argued.

They were strange coins, though. Large old reddish cents, like the ones from the colonial years. The surfaces of the coins were porous and a bit rough with age, but you could easily read the raised pictures on them. One was an Indian head. Another featured a horse's head and a plow. The words *Common Wealth* were spelled out in fat letters on the back of the latest coin she'd spent in his store.

"Pennies from off the eyes of the dead is what they are," Mrs. Moody warned her husband. "She's a ghost that's been robbing the graves next door to hers."

"All she wants is a piece of candy and a little milk," he said. Moody was becoming fond of his antique coin collection.

"No, dear husband. She wants much more than that."

"Why, the milk's for a kitten, I'll wager you. The lady has a pet cat. I'll give back every one of these coins if she doesn't have a cat she's feeding."

Moody spoke with confidence, but he feared his wife might be on to something. He decided to follow the frail customer the next evening when she left his store. She always came at closing time anyway.

That evening she paid for her milk and piece of candy with a large copper coin that had the words *Nova Caesarea* in raised letters on one side. On the other side was a shield and the words *E Pluribus Unum*. It was good American money, after all. He put the coin in its place with the others.

Moody watched from the store window as the woman in the thin, gray dress walked along the length of his porch and down the wooden steps on the far end. She carried the cup of milk in front of her in one hand. She kept the piece of hard candy in her other hand in a fist held tightly at her side.

Moody went out the back door. He almost missed seeing her pass down the road. For being barefoot, the frail wisp of a woman walked swiftly along and was soon over the next hill. He had to run to keep up. Moody followed her to Gunnings Cemetery.

His wife was right, he thought. He'd been taking money from a ghost. But wait! Maybe she was just walking through the burial plots as a shortcut to her cabin. Moody didn't want to, but he followed her into the cemetery.

Gunnings Cemetery is situated on a large hillside that slopes off into a wide cove, with steep, wooded hills rising alongside the other half. Moody watched the woman glide along in front of him to the back limits of the cemetery. The summer moon hung over the trees, but there was still daylight enough for him to see where she was going. She sunk right into the ground and disappeared.

He'd seen enough. Moody ran home. He told his wife. She told her two sisters. Someone told the sheriff. Someone else told Moody's brother. Before long, a crowd had gathered at the store.

"Don't eat another pickle unless you mean to pay for it," Moody told his brother. "We're running low."

"I can get you all the pickles you need," his brother said. "Susan put four dozen jars of 'em in brine."

"That, I did," Moody's sister-in-law said. "We'll bring a jar by Tuesday."

"Save them for your children," Moody said, giving in. "I don't suspect I'll run out of pickles that soon."

"We better look at the spot where she went down," the sheriff suggested. "If it's an unmarked grave, we better see what's what. I haven't been to no funerals for a month or more and the last one was old man John Topp's. Had a white beard growed down to his trousers, he did."

The sheriff brought a lantern. Moody and his brother carried shovels. The women huddled in a cluster of excited whispering as they walked the road to Gunnings Cemetery.

Moody showed them the exact place she disappeared. "She sunk right into the earth," he said. There was a mound of soft dirt encircled by grass. The mound had, in fact, been recently dug, perhaps within the week. Shoveling away the dirt was an easy task.

At the bottom of the grave they found a pine casket. It was a homemade pine box with a lid. Someone must have died up in the hills behind the cemetery. Someone had buried their own without a preached-over funeral. It wasn't unheard of. People caught sick and died quickly from time to time.

The sheriff held the lantern down into the grave while Moody and his brother pried the lid off the casket.

She was inside. It was the same frail woman that had been coming to Moody's store.

"For the love of God," Moody said. "It's her."

She looked more dead than usual. The shriveled corpse wore the thin, gray dress that was ragged at the hem. Her hair flowed down from her head in long dark tangles. Her eyes were closed in death, her mouth drawn tight against her teeth. The chipped teacup was at her side.

"May the Lord have mercy on her soul," the sheriff said. "Is that a sack she's holding in her arms?"

It wasn't a sack, exactly. The corpse held a newborn baby wrapped in swaddling. The baby was alive.

The women gasped upon the discovery.

"She's been getting the milk for the baby," Moody said.

Coffin babies were believed to have happened in history, when a mother died in delivery, before the baby was born. That was the likely case in this instance. The mother was buried, thoroughly dead, and sometime after the baby came into the world to find scant little room, no light, and only a tiny bit of air.

"It can't be alive," Susan said. "I don't believe it."

The baby was most certainly alive. It snuggled to its mother's chest, held tightly inside the dead woman's arms.

"Pull it free," Moody's brother said.

Moody tried. He couldn't manage it.

His brother set aside his shovel to help. One tugged at the baby. The other pulled on the corpse's arms. For all their labor, they couldn't free the infant child.

"She won't turn loose of it," the sheriff said. "But surely a mother wouldn't want her baby to die in the grave with her."

"She's worried for its well-being," Moody's sister-in-law supposed. "I'll give it a home. I'll adopt that baby as my own and raise it proper. What's one more to feed when you have six already? We'll adopt it, won't we, husband?"

Moody's brother agreed they would.

Upon Susan's offer, the dead mother's arms fell away. The corpse released her hold on the baby.

"Praise God," the sheriff said.

Moody lifted the baby from the grave and handed it to Susan, who accepted it readily.

"Why, look here," she said. "It has a piece of candy it's sucking on. Isn't that sweet?"

Moody and his brother put the pine lid back on the homemade coffin. They closed the grave, packing the dirt down good with their shovels. Susan sang a lullaby to her new baby. It didn't seem to mind hearing it.

The people present agreed to tell no one the origins of Susan's youngest, lest the baby grow up to be shunned. County records show a birth registered to Susan Moody that year. The gender of the child and its name are listed there.

Moody expected her back sometime, but the frail woman in gray never returned to his store. When he opened the box of antique pennies the woman had given him, he was surprised by what he found there. The coins were gone. And in their place were golden oak leaves, as many leaves as there had been copper coins. Moody had been bewitched by the woman's ghost.

He ran his store till he died an old man. Warrior's Path State Park is nearby. Park ranger and naturalist Marty Silver has located Moody's old store at the intersection of Old Mill Road and Childress Ferry Road. Although no longer in use, the building was still standing as this story was being prepared for publication. Gunnings Cemetery is still in use and is located near Exit 66 off Interstate 81 between Kingsport and Blountville.

Trick or Treat

from *Ghost Dogs of the South*
by Randy Russell and Janet Barnett

Mrs. Hammond Singleton was crazy, and so was her dog. Every kid in the neighborhood knew it. Her front yard in the Belmont Hillsboro area south of Vanderbilt University in Nashville, Tennessee, was entirely planted in clover instead of grass. She wore a bonnet whenever she went outside. An eleven-year-old in 1962 needed no more evidence than this to be convinced that the old lady was certifiably insane.

Mostly, though, Cindy Linn's grandmother went bonkers on Halloween. She handed out apples to children who came to her door for treats. Not candied apples. Just apples. And that was only the beginning.

Mrs. Hammond Singleton kept a sack of acorns by the door, and every pirate, ballerina, fairy princess, and baseball player who came to her porch on Halloween had to reach into the sack and pull out an acorn and show it to her. Cindy's grandmother would read each child's fortune by looking closely at an acorn, upon which she could see a face, she said, but only on Halloween. Cindy's grandmother held a lighted candle in one hand, by which to study the acorn in her other hand. She recited a poem while squinting at each one: "On All Hallow's Eve, /When the hour is very late, /Find an acorn in the garden. /Upon it read your fate."

"She's nuts," Cindy complained to her mother. "And so's Preston. He follows us to every house. He's always bumping into us. It isn't fair."

Preston was Mrs. Hammond Singleton's Boxer. The dog had the run of the neighborhood. He liked Halloween more than Cindy's grandmother did.

Cindy was a beatnik this year. She wore a black beret, black tights, and one of her father's sweatshirts that came to her knees. She tied a red scarf around her neck and was allowed to wear her mother's lipstick. She didn't know for certain if beatniks wore lipstick. But Halloween was the only time Cindy was allowed to wear it, and she certainly wasn't going to pass up the opportunity to wear lipstick on a night when she might see Ernie Rousch from across the street. Ernie was almost thirteen.

"Having a dog behind me all night doesn't go with my costume, Mom."

Preston knew all the stops. He knew most of the kids in the neighborhood, too. His daily routine, as soon as Mrs. Hammond Singleton let him out of the house, was to secure the entire area. He made a series of rounds each day, six blocks in one direction, six in another, four this way, six that, and back.

Preston was a solitary inspector. He made sure every mailbox was in place. He checked the trees and bushes to see if they were growing as they should. He counted the bicycles, tricycles, and water sprinklers left on the lawns. He saw that the right cars were home and that the right cars were gone. He verified that the rolled newspapers that wouldn't be picked up until the end of day were where they should be.

Dogs in fenced backyards along his route barked as Preston came by. They said hello or alerted him that small pieces of neighborhood were already ably guarded. Preston took down the information as a mental note but never barked back. He had work to do. He was too busy to play.

At one house, he was given a dog biscuit. The young housewife was there every day. If she wasn't, the dog biscuit was sitting on her concrete step as a signal to Preston that everything was okay. In front of another home, a large tabby cat waited in the middle of the sidewalk. When Preston came by, the cat hopped up and followed him to the end of the block, keeping a respectful distance.

Preston possessed a deep sense of community responsibility. And he dearly loved Halloween. It was the one night of the year when people went out to learn his job. He was pleased to accompany them, even if the children were noisy and slow to learn. They couldn't go sixteen steps without eating something.

When children stopped to tie a shoe or repair the rubber band on a mask, Preston hurried back to check on them. He'd even push them a little from the side if they took too long. Then it was important that he catch up to the front again. He would brush by others on the sidewalk to get to the place where he'd left off.

Preston followed Cindy and her friends every Halloween, bumping them when they went too slow, cutting them off if they tried to overlook a house. He'd hurry to the front door to show them where they were going. Then he'd fall back, bumping them once again, and wait on the sidewalk until they had learned the people who lived there and counted the things in the yard.

It was a marvelous job, really. And no dog was better prepared for Halloween duty than Preston. On top of which, being a white-chested, light tan Boxer with black markings, including the traditional black around both eyes, he already had a mask.

Cindy was instructed that she was not only going to her grandmother's house this Halloween, she was going there first.

"She's looking for you, and you aren't going to make her wait, young lady."

"There's bees in her yard," Cindy complained, using up her last excuse.

"Not at night," her mother said. "And they won't bother you anyway, if you stay on the sidewalk."

When she was thirteen, she wasn't doing this anymore, Cindy decided.

She hiked all the way to her grandmother's house with Brenda and Julie, her two best friends.

"She'll ask you to sing," Cindy warned them.

But Brenda and Julie had been to Mrs. Hammond Singleton's before on Halloween. They knew the routine. If you didn't sing, you had to dance to get a treat. If you didn't want to dance, you could get your treat by standing on one foot with your eyes closed.

Brenda and Julie stood behind Cindy when the door opened.

"Hi, Grandma. It's me," Cindy said.

Mrs. Hammond Singleton held the candle out in front of her as if she couldn't believe her eyes.

"Cindy?" she asked. "Are you sure it's you? I thought it was a movie star."

Preston waited inside the door while the three girls chose acorns and had their fortunes told. Cindy would marry a man with a mustache and have eight children, four boys and four girls. Brenda would marry a sailor and have four children, all girls, who would marry sailors when they grew up. Julie would marry a preacher and live in a foreign country. India, Mrs. Hammond Singleton thought it would be, but she wasn't sure it might not be China or Pakistan. They stood on one foot with their eyes closed while Cindy's grandmother dropped an apple in each of their sacks.

"Thank you, Grandma," Cindy said.

"Don't go by the church tonight," Mrs. Hammond Singleton advised the girls. "Circle back the other way. The ghost doubles of those who are doomed to die during the coming year parade through the churchyard on Halloween."

"Okay," Cindy said. "We won't."

Preston trotted out the door as Cindy and her friends walked back to the street, giggling. The fortunes weren't real ones. They were going to marry Elvis Presley, if they married anyone. Or maybe Ernie Rousch. He was almost thirteen and could probably grow a mustache if he wanted to.

Preston went to work counting houses. He took note of trick-or-treaters coming from the other direction. He crossed the street to take inventory, double-checking on the littlest children. Preston liked the littlest ones the best. They worked hard at it, with serious intent, and didn't lollygag like the older kids. Once the newcomers were accounted for, Preston ran to catch up to Cindy and her friends.

Preston bumped into Cindy to let her know he was there.

"Cut it out," she said.

They were getting close to Ernie's house. That summer, Cindy had written her and Ernie's initials in chalk on the sidewalk in front of his house. It was the bravest thing she'd ever done. If he were there tonight, he would see her in lipstick.

Ernie wasn't home, but the girls could peer into the living room through the front window. They saw the couch where Ernie sat when he was home.

"Ask to use the bathroom," Julie said.

"No!" Cindy squealed. "You ask."

When they reached the next block, the girls talked about going back to Ernie's house. He might be home by then.

In the middle of the block, a second-grader had dropped his sack of candy in the street. His older brother was already at the door of the next house. The little guy tried to pick up every piece of candy on the pavement. His Halloween mask made it a difficult task. But he wasn't leaving any. The seven-year-old had worked hard for his treats.

Preston bumped Cindy again. This time, he was trying to get around her to the street. He was the only one who heard the car coming.

Cindy spun around to watch him. She'd never seen Preston run so fast.

Preston rushed with his head low and smacked hard into the little boy, who was bent over on his hands and knees. The Boxer hit the second-grader in the chest and pushed hard until his head was under the boy's stomach. The sack hastily refilled with candy went flying. So did the little boy. He landed on his bottom six or seven feet from where he'd been when Preston made contact. It hurt.

The car hit Preston squarely. It squealed its brakes. The thud was loud and certain. Cindy saw it all. She screamed.

Parents separated themselves from the trick-or-treating children and ran to the street. Several had flashlights. The driver was a college student. He was quick to open the door. The little boy wailed.

"I didn't hit the kid," the driver said.

The seven-year-old was swept up by one of the adults.

"He's okay," the man holding him said. "Just scared. You're okay, aren't you, cowboy?"

"I didn't hit the kid," the driver said again. "I hit the dog."

Cindy ran to the front of the car, looking for Preston. He hadn't made a sound. He was surely dead or badly injured and about to die. She was afraid to find him, to see him crushed, but she had to. She looked to the front of the car, then to the left and to the right. He wasn't anywhere.

"He must have run off," someone said. "Dogs do that sometimes when they get hit. He's probably okay, then. He probably went home."

Cindy was crying. It was a horrible Halloween.

"He saved the little kid's life," Brenda said.

"Everyone saw him do it," Julie added. "We all did."

Cindy hurried home to tell her parents that Preston had been hit by a car. They'd have to look for him. Brenda and Julie came inside with her. They would help look. Brenda could call her father, and they could use his car.

"That won't be necessary," Cindy's mother said. "Are you sure it was Preston, dear?"

"Yes," Cindy said. "He came with us from Grandma's house. He was with us the whole time, like always. This little boy was in the street, and Preston ran ninety miles an hour and knocked him out of the way, and then the car hit him. It hit him real hard, Mom. Everyone heard it."

"You're sure it was Preston? You all saw him?"

The three girls nodded.

"Maybe he's back at Grandma's house. Can you tell her, Mom? Please. I just can't."

"I thought she might have told you, dear," Cindy's mother said. "I imagine she didn't want to ruin your Halloween. Preston had cancer. He died at the vet's yesterday."

Almost fifty years later, there are still trick-or-treaters in the Belmont Hillsboro neighborhood of Nashville who get bumped by a dog if they go too slowly from house to house or stand too long in the middle of the street. An old woman who was a young housewife in 1962 leaves a dog biscuit on the concrete step in front of her house once a year. On Halloween.

The old woman makes the children sing or dance for her, or at least stand on one foot with their eyes closed, before she gives them a treat. She says she learned to do this from an old widow named Mrs. Hammond Singleton, who immigrated to this country from York, England, and who was as crazy as bees in clover. And so was her dog, Preston.

The Shriek of the Banshee

from *Seaside Spectres*
by Daniel W. Barefoot

Extreme fear can neither fight nor fly.

William Shakespeare

One of the most terrifying figures of the supernatural world is the banshee, the messenger of death. After all, there is little more frightening than a symbol of death that imparts a dark and dire warning to its human witnesses: "As I am, so you shall be."

This female spirit is rarely seen. Rather, it is known for its haunting wail, which sends chills down the spines of all those who hear it. On the rare occasions when the banshee appears to the human eye, it takes the form of a young woman with flowing blond, white, or auburn hair. Most encounters with the harbinger of death occur in the late evening or early morning.

While the banshee is most often heard or seen at the birthplace of the person who is soon to die, it is also commonly found at or near well-known geographic landmarks, such as rock outcrops and rivers. Throughout history, most banshees have been associated with Scotland and Ireland. Few have been recorded in the United States. Even rarer is the banshee found in the annals of North Carolina folklore. Since Revolutionary War times, however, the banks of the Tar River near Tarboro, the seat of Edgecombe County, have been home to one of the most legendary of all banshees.

Most North Carolinians are familiar with the graphic scenes of flooded downtown Tarboro in the fall of 1999, after the Tar River poured out of its banks in the wake of the torrential rains occasioned by Hurricane Floyd. Almost twenty-two decades earlier, the Tar was less threatening, its dark, lazy waters controlled by a dam that disappeared long ago. Yet at that time, war was being waged in North Carolina. It was against this backdrop that the Tar River banshee made its first appearance.

Dave Warner, a native of England who had adopted the North Carolina colony as his home, operated a gristmill on a curve of the river below the dam. An avowed Patriot, he supported the cause of independence by providing grain and the use of his mill to the American army. From dawn until late into the night, the mill wheel turned continuously to produce badly needed foodstuffs for hungry Tar Heel soldiers.

Warner, a giant of a man, had black hair and a black beard that were often discolored by the copious flour that he produced. His massive arms and wrists enabled him to handle heavy sacks of grain all day long. There seemed to be no limit to his energy and his drive to win the war.

About high noon one hot, muggy day in August 1781, Warner was hard at work at his mill when he heard the sound of galloping horses. An informant suddenly appeared to warn him that the approaching horsemen were British troopers. "Close your mill and hide," the messenger implored. "The British know you for a rebel, and they will kill you."

Undaunted by the threat, Warner flexed his muscles and replied in a voice of defiance, "I'd rather stay and wring a British neck or two."

In one last attempt to dissuade him, the frightened courier admonished, "But you can't stay and fight a whole army single-handed."

In a calm, matter-of-fact manner, the burly mill owner responded, "I'll stay and be killed. What is my life?"

When the red-coated visitors arrived, Warner and the messenger were busy putting meal in sacks as the big wheel churned the river water. Six British soldiers bounded through the door, but the miller pretended he did not see them. To his young helper, he spoke words meant for the ears of the intruders: "Try to save every precious ounce of it, my lad, and we'll deliver it to General Greene. I hate to think of those British hogs eating a single mouthful of gruel made from America's corn."

Outraged by Warner's insolence, the soldiers savagely assaulted him. Although he fought with all his might, he could not overcome the five men who pinned him to the floor. Warner was not intimidated by their threat to drown him in the swirling waters of the Tar. He countered with an ominous warning: "Go ahead, go ahead, but if ye throw me into the river, ye British buzzards, the banshee will haunt ye the rest of your life, for the banshee lives here. When the moon is dark and the river's like black ink, and the mist is so thick ye can cut it with a knife, ye can see her with her yellow hair falling about her shoulders, flitting from shore to shore, crying like a loon. As sure as the stars are in the sky, if ye drown me, she'll get ye."

Taken aback by the miller's strange harangue, the Redcoats whispered among themselves. "Let's wait until the commander arrives," the tallest of them reasoned. "He will decide for us."

One of his compatriots quickly voiced agreement, but another, a rather large fellow with evil eyes, uttered a profanity and urged immediate action: "Why wait? We are sent on ahead to make the way safe. We'll get rid of this rebel before he makes trouble."

His words convinced two other soldiers to haul the miller down to the edge of the Tar. There, the Redcoats bound his arms and weighted his body with a heavy rock around his neck and another around his feet. Without hesitation, they then threw him into the dark water. As he sank, a bloodcurdling cry—the wail of a woman in pain—echoed along the banks of the river.

Overcome by fear, the soldiers watched in astonishment as a thick mist rose above the water. Before their very eyes, it took the shape of a woman with long hair, just as Dave had warned. Two of the men screamed in terror, "The banshee!" But the cruel soldier with the evil eyes was so frightened that he hurried back to the mill without saying a word.

The blackest kind of night had shrouded the river by the time the commanding officer and the main force of British soldiers arrived at the mill. They established an encampment along the river. While the enlisted men sat around fires near their tents, the officers enjoyed the relative comfort of the mill house.

A thin, yellow moon broke through the clouds and cast an eerie light over the entire campsite. Without warning, the stillness was broken by the unmistakable shriek of the banshee. All of the officers and most of the men rushed down to the river. Cowering inside their tent with their hands covering their ears were the soldiers who had taken part in the miller's murder. Once again, a misty cloud formed above the water and took the shape of a woman with flowing hair and a veil-covered face. All the while, the terrible wail reverberated up and down the river.

Filled with fear and guilt, the murderers related the events of the day to their commander. Disgusted by their conduct, he punished them by ordering them to remain at the mill, where they would work and be forced to endure the ear-piercing cries of the banshee.

After the army departed, the unfortunate men served out their sentence until one night when the banshee left the river and appeared in the doorway of the mill house. There, the soldiers witnessed a ghastly sight as the tall, misty figure flung back her veil and revealed a hideous face. Two of the men followed the banshee as it floated back in the direction of the Tar. At the river's edge, both stumbled and fell into the dark water, never to be heard from again.

As for the trooper with the evil eyes, he remained crouched in fear in a corner of the mill house. On that night, he went mad. He fled into the surrounding forest, where he called out the name of the miller. Within days, his lifeless body was found floating face up at the very spot in the Tar where he had sent Dave Warner to his death.

Since that time, August has remained a haunted month along the banks of the Tar River in Edgecombe County. And so this tale ends with a word to the wise: Avoid an August visit to the river, particularly on a moonlit night. Otherwise, you might hear an agonizing cry and see the ghostly form of the Tar River banshee—the portent of death itself.

Ghostly Legacy of the Swamp Fox

from *Piedmont Phantoms*
by Daniel W. Barefoot

Remember thee!
Ay, thou poor ghost, while memory holds a seat
In this distracted globe.

William Shakespeare

Winding south from its headwaters at the Moore County-Richmond County line to its junction with the Pee Dee River just south of the South Carolina line, the majestic Lumber River is one of the most unspoiled waterways in all of North Carolina. Much of the shoreline of this 125-mile, free-flowing, blackwater river is as undeveloped as it was when America was fighting for its independence. Snaking along the Robeson

County line, the southern quarter of the river offers spectacular vistas of cypress gum swamps and bottom-land hardwoods within the confines of Lumber River State Park.

General Francis Marion, one of the most legendary heroes of the American Revolution, is most often associated with the lowlands of South Carolina. But on occasion, the Swamp Fox and his guerrilla warriors set up camp in the swamps along the Lumber River in Robeson County. The ghosts of a man and woman who died on the gallows at one of Marion's camps here are said to linger near the river.

At the outbreak of the Revolutionary War, the Highland Scots who had poured into southeastern North Carolina faced a dilemma: should they honor the Oath of Culloden and maintain their allegiance to the British Crown, or should they fight for the freedom of North Carolina and the other colonies? The majority of these Highlanders chose to remain loyal to Great Britain. This chilling story of two lovers, Walter Jenkins and Jean McDougald, recounts the ghostly consequences when such loyalties were tested.

One day, deep within a South Carolina swamp near the North Carolina line, Joan and Walter shared a romantic embrace. Walter whispered to her, "I've taken a great chance in meeting you. If Marion's men knew, it would mean my life."

Joan shuddered to think of the risks Walter was taking because of his love for her. On several occasions, the handsome young man, considered one of the best noncommissioned officers in the Swamp Fox's command, had given Joan's father, an avowed Tory, important information about planned attacks by General Marion.

As he prepared to depart, Walter kissed her and said, "I must go. They mustn't suspect me at camp."

Determined to obtain the intelligence needed by her father, Joan called out in desperation as Walter mounted his horse, "Wait! Walter, if Marion plans a raid, please let me know. We are prepared for whatever may happen. Last night, Father said that upon the enemy's next move, we will go to North Carolina."

Walter acknowledged her request and rode off into the darkness.

The next night, Joan was awakened by an owl-like hoot, Walter's pre-arranged signal. She hurriedly dressed and hastened to his side.

Joan had never before seen such a look on his face. His eyes expressed concern bordering on fear, and his voice was filled with desperation. "Joan, you must hurry!" he said. "Our forces are massed for an attack on the settlement. Marion plans to be here by noon tomorrow!"

Joan could muster only a short sentence before Walter climbed back upon his horse: "I must tell Father."

Walter bent down from his saddle to hug her. "May God protect you," he declared.

As the sergeant galloped away, Joan sounded the alarm to Captain Sam McDougald—her father—and the other Tories at the temporary settlement. Before daybreak, they were on the move to North Carolina. Once across the line, the Highlanders settled in a swamp located between the Lumber and Waccamaw Rivers at a place still known as Tory Island. There, they quickly put up a makeshift fort.

Upon learning that General Marion's army had likewise entered North Carolina, Captain McDougald was anxious to receive details of the enemy's whereabouts. Calling his daughter to his side, he implored, "Take a fast horse, Joan. Slip into the camp of the Whigs and persuade the sergeant to warn of his assault."

"But Father, I fear for his safety," Joan pleaded. "At our last meeting, he told me Marion suspected someone of giving information. And I know it must hurt him to betray his superiors."

Confident that he would prevail, Captain McDougald challenged his daughter's loyalty: "Very well, then, the safety of your rebel lover comes before your loyalty to the clan. God forbid that I should have raised such a daughter."

Unable to turn her back on her father and her people, Joan mounted a fleet horse. After riding for miles, she located Marion's camp, where most of the soldiers were asleep. Maintaining a safe distance, the young woman sounded the owl-like signal to Walter. In an instant, he held her in his arms. After a passionate kiss, Sergeant Jenkins asked why she had come to a place of such danger.

"Walter, I want you to save my people," she beseeched. "I have come to you for protection and help. Won't you ride ahead and inform us the hour of Marion's attack?"

Walter agreed, though he feared it might cost him his life.

Tears of gratitude poured from Joan's eyes as she pulled Walter close. "Thank God," she sobbed. "We are too few to fight but too many to die."

Before the infatuated pair took leave of each other, Walter announced his plan: "Have your father put guards on the trail leading to the island. If an order to attack is given, I will ride and tell them for your sake. You must leave now."

When the Tory guards went to their posts along the trail the following night, Joan stayed in a tent along the route in order to see Walter if he brought news of the attack. Midnight came and went, but there was no sleep for Joan. Finally, in the early hours of the morning, one of the guards came to the tent and informed her that a horseman was in the nearby clearing.

The full moon offered just enough light for her to recognize Walter. She rushed to him as he was dismounting. In a frantic voice, he said, "Joan, Marion plans."

Those three words were all he spoke before a round of gunfire provided a violent interruption. Marion's soldiers poured out of the darkness from all sides. "Traitor!" their leader screamed.

Sergeant Jenkins was taken into custody. As he was being led away by the Patriots, Joan found herself overcome with emotion and guilt. Tearfully, she cried out, "Oh, Walter, what have I done?"

General Marion soon launched a savage attack on Tory Island, during which his warriors razed the fort and houses there. In the aftermath of the assault, Captain McDougald and his fellow Scots returned and established a temporary camp at the site.

Poor Joan, suffering from remorse, could not be left alone for fear that she might harm herself. Her mental state approached madness. She constantly saw Walter's face, and the sounds of owls gave her false hope that he was calling her. At length, Joan could tolerate her misery no longer. Under the cloak of darkness, she stole away from Tory Island and rode through the wilderness to Marion's camp in the swamps along the Lumber River. Dismounting from her horse, she approached quietly until she saw that the camp had been abandoned.

But what the Swamp Fox had left behind was horrifying. The bright moon, shining down like a spotlight, revealed a recently constructed scaffold. Swinging from a rope was a lifeless body—that of Sergeant Walter Jenkins.

Joan screamed at the garish sight and stepped onto the platform. Gathering up a piece of rope, she fashioned a noose and joined her lover in death on the gallows.

Even now, when the moon beams down on the Lumber River in Robeson County, it is said that two ghostlike figures can be observed in the swamp at the site of the Swamp Fox's former camp. One of the apparitions is thought to be the ever-faithful Walter, pledging his love, and the other is Joan, pleading for forgiveness.

The Evil Eye

from *Haints of the Hills*
by Daniel W. Barefoot

Evil enters like a needle and spreads like an oak.

Ethiopian proverb

Begun in 1936 as part of President Franklin D. Roosevelt's economic recovery program, the Blue Ridge Parkway is an elongated national park that has as its centerpiece a magnificent roadway along the crest of the Blue Ridge Mountains. From its beginning at Shenandoah National Park in Virginia, the route stretches 469 miles to Great Smoky Mountains National Park in North Carolina and Tennessee. More than half of its mileage is in North Carolina.

One of the many visitor centers located along the parkway is a small facility at Milepost 451.2 in Haywood County near its border with Jackson County. It stands in the shadow of Waterrock Knob, a majestic 5,718-foot peak. From the center, a trail leads hikers on a strenuous climb to the top of Waterrock, where, on clear days, they are treated to a spectacular 360-degree view of the Blue Ridge, Cowee, and Balsam ranges to the east and south, the Smokies to the west and southwest, and Mount Mitchell fifty miles to the northeast.

Few people who enjoy the awe-inspiring beauty of Waterrock Knob realize that the mountain overlooks the former cabin site where one of the most haunting tales in North Carolina history was played out in the distant past. Indeed, one of the principal players in that macabre drama may still haunt the mountain.

Oconee Sheen was fifteen years old when it all began. She lived in a crude cabin at the base of Waterrock with her cruel father, Peter Sheen. They both had thick, reddish hair. But in most every other respect, the two had nothing in common. In fact, Oconee hated her father.

Any love she ever felt for the man had evaporated years earlier when her beloved Cherokee mother, Alca, was laid to rest on the mountainside amid the blooming rhododendron, honeysuckle, and mountain laurel. At the grave site, Peter Sheen had offered an outburst of laughter for every tear that Oconee shed. Following Alca's burial, Peter abused Oconee both verbally and physically. On one occasion, he threw her to the floor, causing permanent damage to her back. But the worst was yet to come. In a fit of rage one dark day, Peter Sheen administered a savage beating with his leather whip. One of the wicked lashes caught Oconee's right eye, causing such irreparable damage that it had to be removed. Oconee filled the cavity of her lost eye with a large, radiant gemstone. But the teenager knew she would forever be disfigured and would never be a woman of striking beauty like her mother. Day by day, her contempt for her father intensified.

Finally, in the stillness of a dark mountain night, Oconee took an ax and hacked her father to death while he slept. She then pulled up the boards of the cabin floor, threw the bloody body of Peter Sheen under the dwelling, covered it with dirt, and replaced the flooring. Oconee walked outside and breathed the fresh mountain air. She felt no remorse. If anyone inquired about Peter Sheen, she would reply that he had returned to his people. At last, she was free!

Years passed. As Oconee grew older, she became uglier in physical appearance. Even her false eye changed, increasing in radiance. Meanwhile, she developed frightening powers. If she looked at a singing bird, it would immediately fall dead. Her strange eye caused plants to wither and die. When she made her way by neighboring cabins, children ran inside and dogs howled, all in fear of the evil that was Oconee Sheen.

No one ever saw her do any work, yet she never seemed to lack for anything. Whatever she needed, she took with her mysterious powers. Those neighbors who refused her demands paid a heavy price. Down in the valley, old Joe Martin rued the day he did not give Oconee the ham she asked for. The woman cast her bad eye at him, then pointed her index finger at his field of golden wheat, ripe for harvest. It immediately burst into flames. Another incident involved a minister from the tiny Jackson County village of Willits, who visited the Waterrock area once a month to preach to the people there. When he informed Oconee that she was possessed by the devil, she cast her evil eye and pointed a finger at him. The parson fell dead.

Oconee's neighbors looked down upon her as a half-breed. As her reign of terror grew, they made every effort to avoid her. Yet no one was safe. Word quickly spread about little Agnes Murphy, a neighborhood girl. The tiny lass made the mistake of laughing at Oconee's twisted, deformed back. Oconee fixed her evil right eye on the hapless child, pointed her index finger, and spoke some strange words. Agnes tried to call out for help, but instead, she quacked like a duck.

Time marched on. As Oconee's age mounted, so did her hatred and bitterness. Because of her physical disfigurement, she had a great contempt for all things beautiful. She hated men because of the abuse wrought by her father. She hated children because of their happiness and laughter. In short, Oconee hated herself.

One day, she fell seriously ill. Dr. Wayne Morton, a physician from Willits, was summoned to her bedside. A fire was slowly dying in the fireplace as the physician bent to check Oconee's pulse and temperature. As he examined her, his attention was drawn to her right eye, which shone like glistening ice. Before Dr. Morton could say anything, Oconee remarked in a rather matter-of-fact way, "I am dying." When the doctor nodded in agreement, the old woman cackled and offered her final haunting words: "You say I'm dying, but you are wrong. Oconee never dies. Even death cannot keep me in the grave." With that, her good eye closed. Dr. Morton could detect no pulse. As he placed the covers over Oconee, the fire suddenly went out, and the cabin was engulfed in darkness.

Oconee was buried on the mountain beside her mother. Strangely enough, all of her neighbors came to see her laid to rest. But no one sang or offered a eulogy or a prayer. As the crude wooden coffin was lowered into the ground, a cloud covered the sun. A dog howled in the distance.

The day after the burial, Dr. Morton paid a visit to Joe Martin and posed a curious question: "Were you ever close to Oconee Sheen?"

Befuddled by the query, Joe shook his head and said, "I always stayed as far away from her as I could."

Excitement building in his voice, Dr. Morton said, "So did I, until the night I examined her. But that night, I discovered something. You know her eye, the right one?" Joe nodded. "It's a stone, all right," the physician continued. "Why, man, it's a diamond as big as a hickory nut! When I leaned over her, the firelight caught it, and it almost blinded me. All these years, she's gone about the hills with a fortune in that socket." With Joe now hanging on every word, Dr. Morton got to the point: "Yes, and now it's buried out on a lonely mountainside. What shall we do about it?"

Without hesitation, Joe replied, "Go get it. Now, tonight!"

The nighttime sky over old Waterrock Knob was unusually dark when Joe Martin and Dr. Morton arrived at the Sheen cabin. Upon reaching the grave site, the two began digging furiously. But when they reached the coffin and began to lift it out, Dr. Morton thought he heard a voice saying, "Oconee never dies. Even death cannot keep me in the grave."

With great trepidation, the doctor lifted the lid as Joe held the lantern. Both men were greatly relieved to see the body of Oconee just as it had been laid to rest. Nonetheless, it took every bit of his courage for the physician to reach into the casket and pull the diamond from the eye socket.

As he started to move away with the prize, something cold grabbed his wrist. Dr. Morton looked down to see Oconee's fingers clutching him in a death lock. As he stood there, immobilized by fear, the corpse unleashed an awful scream, threw her arms around him, and pulled him into the coffin. Tossing the diamond to Joe, Dr. Morton cried out, "Take it and run for your life while I throttle this fiend!"

Frightened beyond description, Joe Martin took the enormous gemstone and raced to his horse. He heard gurgles coming from Oconee's grave as he galloped away.

When he reached his cabin, Joe rushed inside, locked the door, and covered the windows. As he searched for a place to hide the diamond, one of the windows flew open. A deathly cold wind blew into the cabin. And then he saw Oconee standing in the open window, a gaping hole where her right eye had been. "My eye, give me back my stone eye!" she shrieked.

Fearful of her supernatural powers, Joe threw the diamond to her. She caught it and promptly put it back into place. For a moment, the evil eye looked at him, and Joe believed he was a goner. But Oconee merely disappeared into the darkness.

After a sleepless night, Joe returned to the grave site to look for Dr. Morton the following morning. There was no sign of him until Joe noticed that Oconee's grave had been covered again. Picking up the shovel he had used the previous evening, he carefully removed the earth from the coffin. Slowly, he lifted the lid. Inside was the lifeless body of Dr. Morton. Oconee had buried him alive!

The Sheen cabin was claimed by the elements long ago. And the graves of mother Alca and daughter Oconee—or Dr. Wayne Morton, if you will—can no longer be found in the wilderness. But no grave could hold Oconee Sheen anyway. For all we know, she still roams these mountains, for, as she said, "Oconee never dies."